Beginners' Minyan
A Collection of Short Stories

S. Mark Gadol

First Published in the United States by Clothesline Books

Copyright © 2011 S. Mark Gadol

ISBN: 0-98-375930-8
ISBN-13: 978-0-98375-930-0

For Uncle George

CONTENTS

ACKNOWLEDGMENTS

Special thanks to my wife and family for all their support, to my editor, Judy Sternlight, for her thoughts (www.judysternlightlit.com), and to Shira Golding, of Shirari Industries, for her cover design (www.shirari.com).

INTRODUCTION

When I was 19, my uncle, the only religious figure in my family, died from cancer. My uncle had belonged to an Orthodox synagogue, he spoke Hebrew, he led our family Seders (even at my parents' house), he cringed when my brothers and I innocently asked for cheese dogs when he barbequed, and he had Judaica throughout his home.

I, on the other hand, had been kicked out of Hebrew school and asked not to come back as a condition of my having a *Bar Mitzvah*, I made jokes about the pictures of dead cows in the *Haggadah*, I loved cheese dogs, and the only Judaica in my home growing up was the mostly painted-over *mezuzah* on the front door, which had probably been left by the previous occupants.

But I loved my uncle dearly and his death left me feeling alone. So in a small gesture of remembrance, I stopped eating red meat that wasn't kosher. It was in part a tribute, but in looking at my family, I had also realized that there was no one left to carry the torch and somehow, inexplicably, I found that sad and in need of action.

Soon I kicked non-kosher poultry as well. I started to relearn to read Hebrew (I still don't understand it). I fasted on Yom Kippur and then kept a strict Passover. I became Sabbath observant. I read a few books, took a few classes, but mostly learned about Judaism by falling in with a crowd of people who knew a lot about being Jewish and liked to talk about it.

And now my memories of my uncle and his relationship with Judaism are seen through a more informed lens. While my most meaningful memory of the few Shabbat services I attended with him at his Orthodox synagogue will always be of his concentration when reading the prayers, I now know that, ironically, such concentration is often a sign that someone is afraid to lose a page. Not to mention, the fact that we had driven to and from the service is no longer insignificant. I realize that the Hebrew fluency I thought he had was most likely limited to a few essential blessings learned by heart and several Yiddish idioms -- because I've adopted the same trick. I now see the contradiction in banning cheese dogs at a barbeque where cheese-free dogs are being cooked on Shabbat, as well as the fact that the turkey my father made when we hosted a holiday was *treyf* whether it was on the dinner table, where my uncle wouldn't eat it, or sitting on the counter, where he would pick at it mercilessly.

Disappointed? No. Like me, my uncle took from Judaism what meant something to him, leaving or admiring from a distance that which didn't.

It's through this lens that I look at what it means to be Jewish. It's an awe-inspiring religion, tradition and culture, full of beauty, shtick and hypocrisy. As, I suppose, all religions are.

These ten stories, which are not autobiographical, try to capture some of my observations as I have explored what it means to be a Jew. Some are funny, some are cynical, some might border on apostatical. Whatever you take from them, I hope you enjoy them.

S. Mark Gadol, New York City, 2011

TREYF DAY

Thinking back, I don't know how my mother thought she could have gotten away with it. She sent me to Jewish schools. All our friends were Jewish. Yet, I was raised in a home with no distinction between the will of God and the word of my mother. But not the way you're thinking.

Growing up, I was led to believe that the Torah expressly prohibited me from wearing rhinestones.

The Torah.

Rhinestones.

One year I was laughed out of a classroom for insisting that God prohibited girls from wearing two shades of pink at once. When I told my mother about it, she had me moved to another class.

Of course, I realized later that my mother would just mint religious edicts whenever she felt that real Jewish law had failed her. But as a young girl, I just had the sense that something was wrong.

Finally, when I was twelve, I had a revelation. A classmate invited me to her sleepover party. "Abby," I said in a hushed voice, "sleepover parties are forbidden."

"Show me where it says that," Abby said, tossing her hair and walking away. I stood motionless for several minutes. It wasn't her flippancy that unnerved me -- it was her logic.

When I got home, I asked my mother if I could go to the party. She reminded me that sleepovers are forbidden. Without missing a beat I said, "Show me where it says that." She looked at me for a long time. I could tell that she was thumbing through volumes of law in her head.

She coughed lightly into her hand. I could hardly wait for the permission, the recognition, the apology.

"Jessica, you can't go," she said.

"Why not? There's no law against sleepovers, is there?"

"Correct. There is no law that explicitly forbids sleepover parties. But there is one against gossip. And you can't have a sleepover party without gossip."

Tale bearing and *lashon hara*, "the evil tongue," are, in fact, prohibited. And to bring the matter to rest, she showed me where.

Leviticus 19:16.

That day I realized that my mother was as skillful at exploiting real Jewish law as she was at manufacturing her own; and let me tell you, the body of work at her fingertips was massive. It starts with the Torah. There's plenty of no-can-do in there. Then there's the *Gezeirah*, rules intended to prevent violations of the Torah. She also had the *Mishnah*, the multi-volume transcription of the oral law, and the *Gemara*, the millennia-spanning commentary on the *Mishnah*. The *Mishneh Torah*. The *Hilchot of the Rif*. The *Sefer Mitzvot Gadol*. It's endless. If she needed a "no" when I wanted chocolate, she could find it somewhere. I needed a new tactic. And it wasn't long before I found it. Adolescent defiance, plain and simple.

In high school, I realized that everyone's parents created rules expressly designed to make their kids suffer. Only instead of saying, "because I said so" like normal people, my mother would pull some fourteenth century rabbinical commentary out of her ass.

Hungry for independence and ready to test the consequences of disobedience, I defied my mother, missing the impossible curfews she set for me, and forgetting (on purpose) to tell her which friend I was seeing. Boy, that felt good.

But my mother was nothing if not cunning.

One night, after coming home late, I steeled myself for a big lecture.

"You're late," she said when I walked in.

"I know."

She came over and gently took my shoulders. As she gazed into my eyes, I suddenly wondered if she was about to disown me; I could see her sitting *shiva* for me the way that the Weiss's did for their daughter when she married out.

"It's okay," she said.

"What?"

"You're older now. You can make your own decisions and suffer your own consequences."

I couldn't believe my ears.

"I was just looking out for you," she added.

"I know, mom." I could hardly hold back a smile. "Thank you."

"Because it is my obligation to raise you right."

My urge to smile evaporated.

She held me tighter. "The *Talmud* says it's the obligation of the parent to teach the child to swim. I tried. But don't worry. It's my problem. I'm the failure."

I never missed another curfew.

When I started College, I remember hoping that Columbia would put enough distance between us. But the long arm of guilt knows no limitations and I found that my dorm telephone was actually a monitoring system, much like those ankle alarms worn by people under house arrest. As far as my mother was concerned, if it took me three rings to pick up, I was up to no good. And woe unto me if she got the answering machine. After all, how often could I claim to be studying in the library at two a.m.?

"You were probably out with some boy," she would speculate. The fact that she was sometimes right did not diminish the audacity of her mistrust.

When she did get me on the phone, she often asked about my new college friends. For a long time, I kept her guessing. I had gone out of my way to make friends with kids who were different from me, and ended up with a circle that was so diverse, there wasn't another Jew in the bunch. I was proud of that.

From my friends, I learned about calico and Rob Roys, and that most people don't take Christmas sweaters seriously. In return (although I would argue I still owe them), I taught them the basics of kosher law and the rules of the Sabbath. For some reason they were fascinated with these details. We talked endlessly about them. It took them a while to understand my system of "selective-observance," but I still think I lost them somewhere between boiling a kid in its mother's milk and cold salads served dry.

In the end, they just accepted my squiggly boundaries because all that really mattered to them was that it made sense to me.

In some ways, college was a good thing for my relationship with my mother. It didn't change her behavior and it certainly didn't lead to the liberation I had hoped for, but it did give me some perspective. Thanks to Psych 101, for the first time, I started to consider my mother's behavior rather than just lamenting over how it affected me. By midterms, I had hypothesized that her phony laws were not intrinsically about deprivation; they were about power.

"Here's the thing," I explained to my friend Christine, as we took a study break in a coffee shop one day. If you wanted a stereotype, Christine is your girl. Graduated last year from Saint Somebody's Miracle. Tall and blond, she played intramural soccer. The only thing she lacked was the cross around her neck, which one night she showed me was tattooed to the inside of her thigh.

"My mother never had control over her own life," I said. "She moved around a lot as a kid and my grandfather basically picked her friends. He introduced her to my father and pushed her into marriage. Then my father laid down the ground rules; he decided where they would live, he chose their friends, and he

4

put her on an allowance. My mother ran the house; she shopped, she decorated, and after I was born, I became her biggest project."

Christine nodded, biting into an English muffin.

"My mother's disempowerment manifests as an attempt to exert whatever power she can, which means hoarding dry goods, changing the curtains, and micromanaging my existence. She grabbed the only tools she had available: God and guilt."

"Mine's is God and fear," she offered. It was the first time I had heard Christine speak of her mother in a way that didn't involve the logistics of her arrival or departure. I asked her to go on, but she suggested we get back to the books.

Later in the semester, I told my mother my theory in one of our heated phone calls. I could feel her blood pressure rising. She ordered me to forget the witchcraft I had learned in psychology class. Actually, she said "soothsaying," which is prohibited in Leviticus 19:26.

"Mom," I yelled. "You're crazy." And I slammed down the receiver, enraged and desperate to find a way to lash out at her spiritual jugular.

It wasn't hard.

There is one law that I knew my mother hadn't made up. Its existence is undeniable and there's no room for interpretation. Neither Jew nor Gentile could claim ignorance of it. It was the Big One. The Anti-Mitzvah. Leviticus 11:7.

Pork.

Chops, loin, roast, ham, bacon, flitch, Spam! It doesn't matter. Pig is forbidden -- for real.

So I ate it.

Right before finals, Christine and her roommate Michelle had a few of us over, and we drank wine and ordered Chinese food.

They were eating their usual array of dishes and I had Szechuan tofu and don't-ask-don't-tell egg drop soup. Not kosher, but vegetarian enough. It was still early, maybe 9:30, but I was giddy after a few glasses of wine and several nights of studying.

Michelle mentioned that her mother was coming down from Connecticut the following day. Michelle was like Christine, tall and blond. Only she played lacrosse and was Protestant. So I immediately -- and yes, unfairly -- had a picture in my mind of her silk-scarfed mother appearing in a cloud of Chanel, walking through the apartment with a white glove and the curled lip of judgment.

"Better hide the liquor," I said, taking a sip of wine. "Wouldn't want her to see you having fun."

"More like, hide it if you want some left for yourself," Christine responded quickly. Michelle's face soured.

"Oh Jess, tell us the duck story again," Christine said, turning quickly to me. I looked at Michelle, who was looking down and poking a chopstick into a container.

One thing I learned quickly about my college friends was that they rarely spoke about their mothers, yet they encouraged me incessantly to talk about mine. I guess they somehow lived vicariously through my unfiltered rants.

I never found the "Duck Story" particularly fascinating, but for some reason my friends loved it, howling with laughter like a bunch of five-year-olds each time they heard me tell it.

Without going into details, the story ends with a roast duck stuffed with the "Styles" section of the *New York Times*, four knives stuck in a ficus, and me forbidden to wear mohair.

"Priceless," Michelle said.

"Outrageous," Gwen added. Gwen was another lacrosse player; Catholic with a black boyfriend. Perfect fodder to give a mother palpitations. But I couldn't even tell you if she has a mother. Not a word about her.

"Your mother," Michelle said, pausing for effect, "is the most interesting thing about you. She's insane."

Talk about a punch in the gut. The most interesting thing about me? I lifted my eyebrows. "Yeah, but whose mother isn't?"

I don't know what came over me then, or went out of me for that matter. I took a container that I knew was filled with moo shu pork as casually as reaching for a glass of water, grabbed several strips of meat with my chopsticks, and as my friends shouted and lunged forward to stop me, I put the salty flesh into my mouth.

Silence.

I could feel their eyes on me as I chewed. I think they were waiting to see if my head would explode. I ground the meat in my mouth, trying to isolate the taste of the pork from the brown sauce. It was impossible.

"Was that actually your first time?" Christine asked.

I nodded.

"So, pork virgin," Michelle said, "what do you think?"

"It's okay." I took a big swig of wine as everyone continued to stare.

"There are some spare ribs down here," Gwen said.

That hurt.

"Why can you eat it tonight? I thought pork is never okay," Christine asked.

"I know, but--" I stopped myself. I couldn't believe it. I was about to lie. I was actually about to make up a loophole and instantly learned my mother's trick: it's not that she was knowledgeable; it's that I was ignorant.

"It's not okay," I said. "I just wanted to try it."

"*Ef* your mom. That's what that was," Gwen said.

Christine asked me if I felt different.

I wanted to cry.

I got back to my apartment at around two in the morning and found three phone messages from my mother.

I closed my eyes in the darkness and thought about the pork. I dropped one foot onto the floor to help steady myself in the room. A moment later I banged into the bathroom and threw up.

I sat down on the cold tiles, feeling like I had just won a Jewish Trifecta: guilt, embarrassment, futility. What did my friends think of me? And God! What was I going to tell my mother?

I threw up again.

Screw her, I thought. Gwen was right; it was a big smack in her face. And I hope it hurt.

The phone rang at 7:34 the next morning. My mother's voice boomed out of my answering machine, announcing the time and wondering aloud how I could have been out so late on a school night.

I rolled onto my back and rubbed my eyes. I reached from my bed to jerk the curtains open and looked out the window. I was laying in a position from which I couldn't see the grimy, redbrick eyesore that is usually framed in my window. All I saw was a big blue sky.

I cried until exactly 8:12. That's when my mother announced her next call. I started for the phone, but decided to let it go to the machine again. What could I possibly say?

Then I realized that she would call all morning if I didn't acknowledge her. I called her back and let her run through the drama of how she *almost* had a drink to calm her nerves and how she was *on the brink* of calling every emergency room in the city. I chickened out of telling her about the pork and just drummed up some remorse for making her worry and let it go.

Then she said. "How about you come home for Shabbat?"

Oh Christ, I thought, she knows.

"I have a test next week."

"So what? You're not going to study on Shabbat, are you?"

"Of course not. It's just that it's such a pain to get there and then back..."

"Don't be ridiculous. I haven't seen you in so long."

I was quiet for a moment. "What are you up to, mom?"

She fumbled a few words and then said, "Nothing?"

"Someone's home from school this weekend, right? Who is it? Alex Schneider?"

She was quiet. She was so busted.

"But he's so nice."

I laughed -- not because it was funny, but because I was relieved. "Mom, I'm not interested in Alex. I've told you that a million times. You're interested in him. Maybe you should date him."

"Me? That's ridiculous."

I could feel her blushing right through the phone.

"Yeah, mom. You obviously have a huge crush on him."

She laughed. I laughed. It was all very weird and somehow reassuring. I agreed to come home.

I spent the day punishing myself. How could I have been such an idiot? I had thrown away nineteen years of plausible Modern Orthodox Judaism and for what? Moo sho pork? I couldn't have sinned with that honey-glazed ham in Martha Stewart's Christmas magazine? No. I threw it all away on three overcooked, MSG-cured, gray nubs of meat from a two-bit Chinese restaurant that had TWO INCHES OF BULLET PROOF GLASS GUARDING THE ORDERING COUNTER!

I went over to Christine's at lunchtime, returning to the scene of the crime. I was relieved to find her alone. I wanted to ask her what she thought of me, but in the end, I didn't have the guts. We just hung around and ate the rest of the leftovers. She didn't offer me anything with pork in it, so I assumed that everything was okay.

As I got up to leave, she asked if I wanted to go a concert with her Friday night. She offered to buy my ticket in advance so I wouldn't have to break Shabbat. It wouldn't have been the first time I had used Christine as a *Shabbat goy*. I felt ridiculous for having taught her that rule. Was she patronizing me?

"I'd rather not do that," I said. Taking a deep breath, I almost launched into a lengthy explanation, but then I realized I had an easier way out. "Actually, I'm going home Friday. But thanks."

When I arrived at my parents' house, the Schneiders were already there. Alex was impressing the hell out of everyone, turning each question about his academics into a story about his well-connected friends. My mother ate it up, lumping scoop after scoop of potatoes on his plate as he talked.

I, on the other hand, turned every question about my friends into a story about my major.

"You're at Barnard, right?" Mr. Schneider asked me.

"No, I'm at Columbia."

"Oh, right. How's the Jewish scene there these days?"

I saw Mr. Schneider maybe three times a year and he always asked the same stupid questions. First, having gone to Columbia, he loved the veiled and misguided insult about Barnard -- Columbia's sister school. Second, he knew the Jewish scene, which hasn't changed since they first let us in.

They looked at me.

"Jessica is expanding her horizons," my mother said while I shoveled string beans into my mouth.

"What she means," my father said, "is that Jessica's not too involved in Jewish life on campus. I think it's good for her."

I put my hands to my head. "I don't understand how this became a discussion."

"I don't know," my mother said shyly. "It just seems so much more difficult to--"

"To what?" my father interrupted. "To stay Jewish? Stop worrying about Jessica." He turned to the Schneiders. "You don't worry about Alex, do you?" They shook their heads violently. I so wanted to tell them about the time in high school when Alex led his all-kosher floor hockey team into a White Castle after a game.

My father turned to me. "Have some faith in the girl. Right, Jess?"

"I promise you," I said, "no matter how many non-Jewish friends I make, I will always be their Jewish friend."

For the next ten minutes the four parents discussed the meaning of my answer as if I had thrown a juicy *Midrash* to a pack of Talmudic-starved Rabbis.

I saw a smile cross my mother's face. It seemed an odd point to bring her such pleasure. But there it was. I would always be my friends' Jewish friend.

Oh, and I ate pork last night, I said to myself, finding it funny for the first time.

I woke the next morning to the sound of a downpour. Looking out my window, I knew that even my mother would balk at the idea of walking to *shul* in this.

But I was going. I may have been able to come to terms with my stupidity, but I still wanted to hedge my bet.

I got dressed, went downstairs, and found my mother sitting in the living room in her robe. I strutted past her a few times while she scrutinized me with skepticism. But her doubt gave way when I put on my raincoat.

"It's a mitzvah to go to *shul* in the rain," I said, half believing it. In fact, I think my mother told me that once.

"You think I don't know that? Wait for me," she said and ran upstairs.

She returned a little later, neatly dressed and made up. She put on her raincoat and cinched the belt, tightening the hood around her head so that only the small box of her features was showing.

I stood up and did the same.

"Ready?" She said.

"Ready."

She opened the door and we both walked out into the pelting rain. Just outside, I stood under a stream of water that overflowed from the gutters of the house, momentarily entranced inside my hood by the sound of the water drumming against the rubber armor. It made me feel like a kid.

My mom squinted up at the sky for an instant as the rain assaulted her face. "It's not so bad."

"Just a drizzle, really," I said. "Ready?"

"Yep."

I reached for her hand and we headed out into the storm.

VILLA PUESTA DEL SOL

"Now that's class," Sadie said, stretching her flabby, liver-spotted arm across me to ladle a matzo ball into her bowl. "Cooking for your own *shiva*."

Daisy reached across me from the other side, spearing a piece of gefilte fish and dropping it onto her heaping plate. For a tiny woman north of eighty, her appetite was huge. "Ardell was something special, that's for sure," she said, in a voice ruined by years of smoking. "It all tastes so fresh."

Tired of being bumped into, I backed up and let the other ladies get to Ardell's buffet table first. It was weird standing in Ardell's home and eating her food, what with her dead and all. Out of respect for her, I decided not to remind everyone she had simply frozen everything, and that Sylvia and I had just heated it up. True, not everyone prepares food for their own *shiva*. But there was no magic to it. The matzo balls weren't even that good.

Her brisket, on the other hand, was amazing.

Personally, I think Ardell cooked for her own *shiva* just so she would be remembered as the woman who cooked for her own *shiva*. She probably stood there, her squat little body leaning over the stove, schvitzing and mumbling to herself about how hot it was -- too cheap to turn on the air conditioner -- and picturing this very day. She even left instructions for what food went

13

where on the buffet table. I noticed that she had rearranged the pictures on her sideboard, putting the old ones of her when she was young in front of the newer ones of her being old. It would have ruined her reputation if I blabbed about all the food Sylvia and I had to throw out because it was obviously made when the brain cancer had started to eat away at her good sense.

Sadie finally finished romancing the string bean soufflé and moved down to the herring, so I cautiously edged in between Doris and Daisy. Some girls are so pushy. Not me.

"Minnie, pass me the salt, will you?" Doris asked me. She was wearing some fancy-schmancy white and gold paisley-print number, her necklaces and bracelets dangling and clanking around. Overdressed as usual. There was no reason Doris couldn't get her own salt, but she just loved bossing people around. Feeling like her servant -- a hungry one, who hadn't eaten anything since breakfast -- I grabbed a salt shaker and handed it over. Doris didn't even say thank you. She just took the shaker, shook out some salt, and then walked into the living room.

Doris thought she was queen of the universe, and as soon as Ardell was gone, she got even worse. The ambulance hadn't even taken Ardell's body from the building when Doris started talking about replacing her at the weekly mahjongg game. That probably made her feel pretty high and mighty at the Villa.

Villa Puesta Del Sol is our retirement complex in Florida. It means Sunset Village in Spanish, although the only nice sunset I can see from my apartment is the sun setting over the ocean on the welcome sign out front. I think they gave it that Spanish name to make it sound exotic. When my dead husband Frank and I first came to look at the place eight years ago in 1975, the name made me think of some resort in Latin America where movie stars and tycoons would go to gamble and drink cocktails. Back then, the Villa was a community exclusively for retirees. But people die, and for some reason there weren't enough old people to go around. So a few people moved in from Puerto Rico or Cuba or wherever else they come from. I didn't mind, really. They do a lot of good services, like manicures and cleaning apartments. Still, once real Latin Americans were living here, the Spanish name sounded a lot less fancy to me. That's a funny kind of thing.

Maria was the only Spanish person at the *shiva*. She was Ardell's cleaning girl. Dominican, I think. I never could tell those places apart. Maria was the only one crying and not eating. I wondered who had thought to invite her. The mahjongg crowd and the Spanish crowd didn't really talk too much.

As soon as their plates were full, Sadie, who moved like a snail, along with Daisy and Pearl, followed Doris into the living room and I was finally able to make up my own plate. I took my time. I dreaded going into the living room.

Ardell's living room was pretty big and it got a lot of light from her balcony doors and big windows that overlooked the pool. It had a baby blue rug and thin white curtains. The room seemed like a cabana to me, open and airy, especially compared with my living room, which was dark and cramped with my stuff. The only thing out of place here was Ardell's old walnut breakfront that everyone always swooned over, but I thought it was pretty tacky. She had a lot of figurines and novelty plates in it. I liked those.

There were about ten chairs in a circle, and some of the girls hung around on the sides talking. Two seats were empty, but I would have had to walk smack through the middle of the circle to reach them. I couldn't stand the thought of everyone looking at me while I walked through. I guess you could say I'm a little uncomfortable in front of people. I never know what to do with my hands. So I took one of Ardell's counter stools from the kitchen and moved it outside the circle and sat down. It was a good seat because it was high and I could see the whole group, and they weren't paying any attention to me.

Or so I thought.

"Nice t-shirt, Minnie," Daisy called out from across the room in that husky voice that gets everyone's attention. Everyone turned to look. Sadie rolled her eyes and Tillie and Marta looked at each other. I thanked Daisy, even though I knew she was being sarcastic. All my life, people have made jokes at my expense, thinking I don't notice. I've always just played along like I'm clueless, which is not at all true, so the joke's really on them. At least that's how I see it.

That t-shirt comment hurt, though. Ardell loved to play bingo so I thought she would have liked that I wore my "bingo" t-shirt to her *shiva*. The word "bingo" was spelled out across the top in snazzy gold letters that swooshed across my chest, and there was a picture of three bingo balls below, which were surrounded by red and white rhinestone stars.

I took a bite of the brisket, which was, of course, fantastic. Ardell was world famous in the Villa for her brisket and as long as we had known her, she had kept the recipe secret. When Sylvia and I went through the kitchen after she died, preparing for the *shiva* and throwing stuff out, both of us were on the lookout for her recipe box. Lucky for me, I spotted it first, and hid it until Sylvia took out the trash. As soon as she was out the door I opened the box and found the brisket card. The recipe was pretty basic, but lo and behold, in the bottom left corner was the secret ingredient. It made me laugh because it was so unexpected that no one ever would have guessed it.

Smucker's grape jelly.

Rather than stealing the whole card, I tore the corner off with the secret ingredient. Reading the tiny scrap one more time to make sure I wasn't mistaken, I popped it into my mouth and swallowed it. Then I replaced the card and stuck the box behind Ardell's cow-shaped cookie jar, where Sylvia soon found it.

Sylvia let out a big "whoop!" and right away, she dug out the card and then laughed out loud. "Wouldn't you know it!"

I put on a good act, telling Sylvia it was wrong to see the secret ingredient, since Ardell would have told us what it was before she died if she wanted us to know. She handed me the card.

"Ardell, you old devil," I said, which I thought was pretty clever.

Sylvia told the women at the *shiva* about finding the recipe card with the corner ripped off. They all laughed and said how that was "so Ardell." Then they took turns guessing at the secret ingredient. Thyme was the ingredient most of them guessed, but that was only because Doris suggested it. As soon as Doris said it might be thyme, suddenly everyone else thought it might be thyme, too. If I had said thyme, they would have all disagreed. But since it was Doris, everyone tasted thyme.

Even before I knew Ardell's secret ingredient, I knew it wasn't a spice. What made her brisket unique was a special sweetness. I had often wondered if it might be maple syrup. Now I was the only person who knew the truth and I felt an urge to shout out, "I've got it! It's grape jelly!" But I had a feeling that keeping the secret ingredient a secret for now was important. Besides, like I said, if I suggested grape jelly, they'd say it was a stupid guess.

Sylvia said we should send a piece of brisket to a lab, like on *Quincy*. I could tell Sylvia was being totally serious until the women had a good laugh. She ended up just laughing along, probably to hide feeling stupid.

I wiped my lips with a napkin, and let a corner slip into my mouth so I could take a tiny bite. I'm not supposed to do that, but sometimes I just can't help it. I look at paper -- especially soft paper, like tissues and napkins -- and I can feel it melting in my mouth.

My sister found out I ate paper when I was ten and she never let me forget it. Her favorite taunt was that I would eat a love letter, although a boy would never send me one. She was right on both counts. No one ever sent me one. And I know for sure that if a boy had, I would have eaten it on the spot. But that's not fair; who ever received a love letter and didn't want to just eat it right up? In any event, my eating paper had a big effect on my childhood. It made everything hard, especially making friends. Not that anyone outside my family knew my secret. But when you're a kid, hiding something embarrassing brings on a lot of shyness; and shyness is just a blush away from loneliness.

I got a bunch of tests for the paper-eating years ago because it drove Frank crazy. The doctor said it was a condition called pica and in my case, harmless. Frank convinced me to try sniffing smelling salts whenever I had the urge to eat paper, figuring I would associate the bad smell with a bad craving. That didn't work. In fact, the reverse happened. Whenever I walked by a bathroom at the mall that smelled of ammonia, I stopped in to eat some toilet paper.

Feeling restless, I went into the kitchen to get myself a fresh drink. When I got back, the women were talking about Ardell's two sons. They had come the other day and set up a nice little service for her in the rec room. We all knew Ardell's sons because they visited regularly from Phoenix and they usually brought her grandkids. The sons had asked Sylvia and me to help clean out Ardell's apartment (because we stayed to help clean up after the service), which is how we found all the food labeled for the *shiva*.

My two boys and my grandkids never really visited me. They were just too busy or the kids were sick or they were going someplace else. They called -- just not enough.

Between my kids not visiting, the pica and my t-shirts, I was on the bottom rung of the Villa's popularity ladder. I spent a lot of time thinking about that. I didn't know any of these women back in high school, but I felt sure that the popular ones now were the popular ones then. You'd think a bunch of women on death's doorstep would judge one another by things other than looks, sense of humor, money and men. Nope. In fact, it's worse because there's nothing else to do. So I figured we were all, in the golden years of our lives, exactly who we'd been in high school. And for me, all the personality I didn't have then I don't have now. I guess trying to change who you are after high school is like an eighteen-year-old dogwood tree trying to turn itself into a maple. You just don't see it clearly until you're old.

The only thing that can temporarily boost your popularity is having your grandkids coming to visit. Since retirees' sons and daughters don't come too often, when they do, you figure the person they're coming to see must be pretty special. Plus little kids are an easy laugh, which makes you feel popular, and they can be bribed to like you with cupcakes. So whenever someone's grandchildren come to visit, everyone hovers by the pool in hundred-degree weather with a Baggie full of sweaty Ding Dongs and crappy old jokes, waiting for the grandmother to come down and parade the kids about.

Oh, and just like in high school, where the popular kids had their table in the cafeteria, in the Villa -- believe it or not -- we had our mahjongg tables.

Some retirement communities are canasta villages. Other developments favor bridge, pinochle or hearts. But at Villa Puesta Del Sol, our passion was mahjongg, which is a game similar to gin rummy, only you use tiles instead of cards and it's much more sophisticated because it's Chinese. Everything for us revolved around mahjongg. There had been a Wednesday night mahjongg game since they first opened the gates. When a Villa woman looked at a calendar, she saw weeks that revolved around Wednesdays. We shopped on Sundays for mahjongg hors d'oeuvres; got the cleaning girl in on Mondays; went to the beauty parlor on Tuesdays; had lunch to discuss the winners on Thursdays. It was like time circled instead of moved forward.

The most popular girls were in the Prime Game, which was the game everyone wanted in on. There are four players in typical mahjongg games. But in our version, one extra person rotated in to accommodate bathroom breaks. The five women in the Prime Game (Ardell, Doris, Greta, Pearl and Sadie) walked around together like a gang -- a silver-haired, pastel and polyester *West Side Story*. For two years, Ardell had hosted the Prime Game, so she had been top dog. When Ardell died, that bitch became Doris.

Ardell had been popular because of her brisket and wittiness, and because her grandkids were always coming to visit. Doris's tactic was meanness. Greta was super popular because her son would fly her to be with his family on vacations all over the world. We figured that if he did that, she really must have been worth liking. Pearl was golden because all the men in the Villa loved her. She would sit out by the pool with her blue polka dot swimsuit and big, white cartwheel hat, looking like a wrinkled Easter egg, and the guys would just flock to her. Sadie was nice, but she was at the Prime Game table for one reason: she was the worst mahjongg player in the Villa. The truth is that when Ottie (who was in the Prime Game before Sadie) died two years prior, the next in line was Sylvia. But Sylvia is a mahjongg dynamo and would have beaten the plaid off Ardell and Doris. So they skipped Sylvia for Sadie. Now that Ardell was gone, Sylvia was back in the running.

While Ardell, Doris, Greta, Pearl and Sadie played the Prime Game on Wednesdays, the rest of us took turns hosting other games. Sometimes it felt like all we talked about at our games was the action at Ardell's. We speculated about what they were saying, what they were eating, what they were wearing. We all had a vision of them in evening dresses, sipping champagne and eating caviar, even though we knew they sat around like the rest of us in textured blouses, eating onion dip and Fritos. That didn't matter. We all wanted in on that table -- bad.

That is why, in the middle of the *shiva*, Sylvia suddenly invited everyone over for tea that Tuesday night. To me, it was a clear attempt to get picked to fill Ardell's spot. Tea? Everyone accepted since there was nothing else to do on Tuesday nights, with *St. Elsewhere* on Mondays and mahjongg on Wednesdays.

I went inside to get more brisket and matzo balls. Pearl was there. I was standing on one side of the table near the pickles, waiting a long time for her to finish making her plate. For a sporty lady, she was taking an awfully long time. It was like she was guessing the calories of every piece of food she picked up. I wished I knew how to make small talk. Looking at Pearl in her fancy black dress, I suddenly felt self-conscious about my t-shirt. I made a little coughing sound and asked her, in a whisper, to pass me a matzo ball.

Pearl said, "Why sure, sweetheart," which made her sound southern, even she was from Long Island -- South Shore, but not the same. She ladled a real big matzo ball into my bowl. I said thank you and she smiled at me. Then she said that she was sure going to miss Ardell. I smiled and nodded. I went back into the room and took my place back on the stool.

The conversation had turned to the condo board, rules about kids swimming in the heated pool, and Consuelo, the Cuban girl who did everyone's nails. Consuelo was pregnant -- father unknown.

After a while, Pearl said she had to change for a tennis match. She started to go around the room to say goodbye. To my surprise, she said, "See you soon, Minnie." I looked up fast and waved. I had some matzo ball in my mouth and swallowed it. "I hope so," I said, which I thought was a pretty calm, cool and collected thing to say.

The *shiva* broke up right after Pearl left. It was like everyone sensed it was time to go or they would end up cleaning the place. Of course, Sylvia and I were the only ones who volunteered. But while I started cleaning, Sylvia took her time herding everyone towards the door, saying that she was happy to stay and help clean (help me, that is, because even Maria was leaving). It was just one more tactic to get herself into the Prime Game.

When everyone except Sylvia was gone, I got to thinking about Pearl making a special point to say goodbye to me. She was a nice lady, but she had never gone out of her way to acknowledge me before. I wondered if there was something special I had done or said when we were at the buffet table. She had said she would miss Ardell. I hadn't really responded to that. The only other thing I could remember was asking her for a matzo ball. She was real nice about that. Even picked out a big one for me.

My brain was noodling on that. It just seemed funny that someone would be nice to you because you asked for a matzo ball. I looked at Sylvia wiping down the counter. She was humming a song and I could tell she was picturing herself in Ardell's spot at the Prime Game. But when I thought about everyone running off and leaving her to clean up, it was more like the joke was on Sylvia.

I picked up a tray of salad and stood in front of the refrigerator. Taking a second to muster my courage and composure, I said, "Sylvia, open the door for me, will you?" She nearly dropped her sponge on the floor rushing over to open the door. I put the salad into the fridge, said thanks, and went back to the other room.

Those two interactions — with Pearl and Sylvia -- somehow made me think about Clair Wasserstein, who cheated off me from the third grade through high school. I loved Clair and she hated me. She called me Minnie Mousey. Yet, come test time, I always let her peek at my paper, figuring that she would like me for doing it. Now, watching Sylvia, I started to wonder if I'd had it backwards all along -- if my helping Clair made me like her more.

I spied a box of cans and jars in Ardell's kitchen. As we finished up, I asked Sylvia if she wouldn't mind me taking the box because I hadn't been to the grocery store in a few days, which was a lie. She could not have been happier to give me the whole thing. Then she just started talking to me, about Ardell, mahjongg, her kids. It was magic.

That night, I had a lot to think about. I pictured trying to make myself more popular and actually felt a little ray of hope. One good thing about living in a retirement community: there's a lot of turnover. A seat at the game, the best parking space, or a spot on the board is just a heart attack, stroke or fall away; you just have to outlast the next guy.

Then I remembered, I didn't just have this one new idea, I also had Ardell's secret ingredient. What if I made a brisket as good as Ardell's? I jotted down a grocery list before going to bed.

Tuesday came and no one had been named to the Prime Game yet. I arrived at Sylvia's at about five o'clock for her tea thing in a t-shirt that read, "A Star is Born," under which were the names Barbra Streisand and Kris Kristofferson, all outlined in rhinestones, as if it were a marquee. The room got quiet when I walked in. But when they saw it was me, the place got noisy again. I heard someone snicker about my shirt. There were about twenty women mingling about. Sylvia had a big apartment in one of the tall buildings in the Villa. I went to the buffet table. There were ladyfingers and some cucumber sandwiches with the crusts cut off, but everything was still under cellophane. I saw Sylvia running around trying to neaten things up. Then I realized that the Prime Game foursome hadn't arrived yet, which was probably why Sylvia hadn't taken the cellophane off the food.

All the women were especially dressed up for a Tuesday and everyone was talking about the open spot in the Prime Game. Any time the front door opened, they rolled toward it as if the floor tilted in that direction.

Sylvia called out to me from the kitchen, "Minnie, dear, could you give me a hand with this?" I didn't know what "this" was, and it was time to test my new strategy. So I asked Letta, who was standing nearby, to help Sylvia in the kitchen since I had to go to the bathroom. I said, "Ask her to forgive me, ok?" It worked like a charm. Letta dashed to the kitchen and Sylvia waved to me. Forgiveness is really just another form of favor, right?

I went into the bathroom so it wouldn't look like I was lying. Sylvia had put a little sculpture made from mahjongg tiles on the sink, which only showed that she was trying too hard. I had purposely not worn my mahjongg t-shirt for that reason, thinking that "A Star is Born" was more subtle. What a great shirt, though. It had mahjongg tiles across the front and the word "mahjongg" spelled out with Chinese-like letters, all written with sparkles.

I came out of the bathroom just as Doris, Greta, Pearl and Sadie arrived. Sylvia ran up to them like a puppy. I noticed that the plastic wrap had been taken off the food and wondered how Sylvia had managed that so fast. As soon as the hors d'oeuvres were uncovered, the room seemed to tilt back and I was hit with a wave of Shalimar as everyone barreled towards the buffet. Sylvia tried to lead the guests of honor to the table but she couldn't get through. Parting the Red Sea must have been easier than getting to a buffet table in a retirement home.

Doris just pushed through, of course.

Once the buffet was picked clean, everyone mingled. By the time I got there, there were a few olives left on the tuna plate and the bottom half of a cucumber sandwich. In one ear I caught Gloria saying, "So, Doris, do you need a fifth for tomorrow night?" Talk about guts. I couldn't believe it. Gloria had obviously gone to the beauty parlor specifically to ask that question. Her hair looked like a stiff bird's nest and she was wearing a little pillbox hat.

I guess everyone else heard her question as well since the room went quiet, except for the clinking of about a hundred bangle bracelets.

Wouldn't you know it, though? Instead of answering, Doris just walked away.

After that episode and with the food all gone, the party got pretty boring. Sylvia tried to keep things lively. She walked around saying, "Isn't this a great party?" It was a little pathetic.

I talked for a while with Lily, who was the only Catholic woman in the mahjongg crowd. Lily was hosting me, Sylvia, and two other women for mahjongg the following night. The last time she'd hosted, she made a really nice spread of snacks, but she also made a Velveeta cheese mold of Jesus on a cross. She called it Cheesus. No one ate it because it seemed kind of awful to smear another person's god on a cracker. But I got to make a joke about a Gouda Buddha and a Chèvre Shiva, which I thought was pretty hysterical.

Lily was telling me about the fun she had with her grandkids, who had visited over the weekend, even though she did what everyone did; she watched the kids swim and then took them to Publix. As soon as she paused to take a breath, I excused myself and made a beeline for Sadie.

Sadie was trapped in a corner by a window, surrounded by a group of women who were talking about upcoming doctor appointments. I sort of reached in, touched her arm, and said, "Excuse me, Sadie, do you have a second?"

Sadie nodded eagerly and we went to a quieter spot. Once there, I said, "Would you tape *Hardcastle* for me? I have a thing to do on Saturday." I knew that *Hardcastle and McCormick* was Sadie's favorite show. Plus it made it sound like I had something to do Saturday night.

"Sorry, Minnie," she said. "I don't have a recorder."

I thought quick. "Well, what do you say I come along with you on your mall-walk on Sunday and you can tell me all about it? I've been meaning to do some walking."

Sadie's face lit up. It stunk for me because it meant I would have to go to the mall at about eight in the morning before it opened. But Sadie was so happy she talked my ear off for fifteen minutes about the kind of walking shoes I should buy.

One down.

I swung by the buffet table again to see if any new food had appeared. Nothing. I grabbed a napkin and took a small bite. I think Birdie saw me, but I really didn't care because Birdie was in the early stages of Alzheimer's.

Frank used to say, "aging is just a bi-product of living," any time something reminded him he was old. What an optimist he was. He wore his age like a medal. Birdie's blank face made me think about those words and I wanted to share them with her, but wasn't sure it would come out right. For a split second I saw her lucidity come back. Then a butterscotch sucker fell from her mouth, like she had just forgotten it was in there.

I moved in on Pearl and Greta who were talking about the Villa's tennis courts with two women who had recently moved to the complex. These two were a little younger, not-yet widowed and they looked pretty spunky in the crowd. It crossed my mind to ask Pearl for tennis lessons, but I knew that if I asked too many people for lessons and mall walking, the exercise would probably kill me. So instead, I asked for an introduction. Greta was happy to oblige and she introduced me as her friend, which was really nice and unexpected. She told them I was a whiz at mahjongg. The girls pretended to be impressed. They were new and had just driven down through the Lenders' Corridor, which is what we call the stretch of I-95 from New York to Fort Lauderdale where you can't find a good bagel. I could tell they hadn't been caught up in the mahjongg craze yet. Then Pearl (of all the well-dressed people) added that I was known for my t-shirts. She said it in a nice way that actually made me feel kind of flattered. I talked to the new women for ten minutes about where they were from and why they moved here (the weather, the lifestyle, the usual). It was pretty boring, but I did a good job pretending to be interested. Then I excused myself to go get a drink.

Three down.

For the first time in my life, I was working a room, and I wasn't half bad at it. I felt so good. World famous in Villa Puesta Del Sol.

Me.

Then I saw Doris. Number four. She was standing across the room talking with Daisy and Gladys. I suddenly felt underdressed again, but I made myself move closer to hear what they were saying. I figured Daisy and Gladys would be buttering her up with talk about mahjongg; but they were talking about jam. Daisy said something about orange marmalade and how she liked the kind with peels in it. Gladys said she preferred orange marmalade without the peels, but that she loved apricot jam the most. I had no idea how they figured that conversation was going to help them get into the Prime Game. Maybe they were teaming up to bore Doris to death so one of them could take her spot and the other could take Ardell's.

Doris was just standing there with a Styrofoam cup of coffee in her hand. She probably asked for the coffee on purpose at the tea party just to be like that. She was staring beyond the two women with a glazed look in her eyes. I noticed that Doris was standing near a stack of napkins on a table. I nonchalantly asked her to pass one. She actually looked grateful to have something to distract her from Daisy and Gladys, who had moved on to jam brands.

She reached out to hand me the napkin. Before I could say thanks, Daisy's husky voice rang out. "Do you want some mustard with that napkin, Minnie?"

I was stunned. Daisy had completely torpedoed my work with Doris, who laughed along. But I kept my cool and laughed a little as well. Then I fought back, which was something new to me. I said, "I'm not hungry right now, Daisy, but there's some cranberry juice over there. I hear that's good for the, well, you know..."

Daisy's face went red. Doris let out a big laugh and almost spilled her coffee. My comment was a low blow, but it was definitely called for. Daisy had some kind of chronic yeast infection, which she always talks about at the pool.

Four down. Almost.

The party broke up just after that. It was about seven fifteen and everyone wanted to get home to watch *Wheel of Fortune*. I couldn't believe that Doris wasn't going to announce who would fill Ardell's spot; the next game was scheduled for the following night! Would they play with only four? While not unheard of, it was sure a big statement and it also meant limited bathroom breaks.

I spent the next morning working to replicate Ardell's brisket. While I couldn't forget the secret ingredient, I had no idea about the measurements. I hoped to get the recipe just right so I could bring a taste to everyone at Lily's that night. After using up the meat I was pretty close, but one batch was just a little too sweet and another not sweet enough. In the end, I made some spinach dip and brought a bag of Fritos.

I got to Lily's a little early, wearing my favorite mahjongg t-shirt (the one I talked about before with the Chinese-looking letters). Lily was still setting up. She thanked me for the snacks and put them at the end of the buffet table, sort of away from the main spread. Her dishes included chopped liver, which she insisted on calling pâté, some fancy crackers, and breadsticks wrapped in bacon, which a microwave salesman showed her how to make in a demonstration. Some mahjongg women had become kind of religious in their old age and wouldn't eat bacon anymore, and they avoided eating at Lily's because they thought she was serving it on purpose because she was so religious the other way. Not me, though. I thought she was harmless and I like her little wraps.

Sylvia arrived, bearing chopped liver, kosher salami and Ritz crackers. Lily put them out on the edge of the table near my Fritos and dip. Ester and Fredda came together. They were having a big laugh because they both brought a Jell-O angel food cake. That cake had become all the rage in the complex. You skewered the cake before pouring on the Jell-O so it dripped into the cake. It was pretty nifty and tasty.

We sat down to the first game, with Ester sitting out.

We racked up the tile walls, which is how you start a game of mahjongg. It's the part I love best. There is something about the cleanliness of the square wall of tiles, stacked two high, and the anticipation of chipping away at it; it looks like a little fortress.

Ethel had an old forty-five of "Since Ma is Playing Mah Jong" by Eddie Cantor and she brought it to every game. She put it on Lily's record player and moved the needle into position. Lily drew dealer and we started to pick apart the wall and put the tiles in our racks.

The record scratched into position and Eddie started to sing in that old phonograph style, sounding way off in the distance: *"Since Ma is playing Mah Jong, Pa wants all Chinks hung."* Ethel was pointing her fingers in the air and doing a little dance in her chair.

Not many people know how to play mahjongg, I won't waste your time with all the rules. Like I said before, it's basically gin rummy with domino-like tiles. One big difference is that when someone discards a tile in mahjongg, she announces the tile she is putting down. Lily dropped the first tile. "Two bam," she said, putting down a tile with a bamboo stalk and the number two on it.

We were off.

Sylvia picked up the two bam, said, "chow," which is a run of three tiles. She then put down a three krak, which is a tile with funny Chinese writing and a three on it.

No one wanted the krak so I drew a tile from the wall. It was a three bam, which I wanted. "Four dot," I said, putting down a tile.

The game was moving. The tiles were clinking away as we slid them into the center or passed them to each other.

"Four bam," Fredda said.

Then it started back with Lily. "North," she said, putting down that tile.

"Well," Sylvia said. "Looks like they're playing with four at Doris' tonight. Five dot. First time that's happened since I don't know when."

I picked up the five dot and put three tiles on the table. "Kong. Yeah, I was surprised. I figured we'd have to replace you tonight, Syl. Five krak."

Sylvia smiled.

"Not me," Fredda said. "I knew Doris would rather watch everyone sweat than to pick the fifth. Eight dot."

"South," Lily said.

"Hey Ethel," I said, as soon as Ethel moved near the buffet. "Could you fix me a little plate?"

Ethel hopped to it.

"My, you're in a good mood," Sylvia said. "Four krak."

"No, not really. Pung. Two bam. Just looking at so many good tiles here makes me a little hungry."

"At least one of us has something," Fredda said. "Eight bam."

"I bet they don't have pâté there," Lily said. "Pung. Two dot."

"No, but I'm sure the chopped liver is excellent," Sylvia laughed. "Flower."

My turn again. "North. Lily, could you reach around and grab me a napkin?"

"I heard that they were having brisket tonight. Sort of in honor of Ardell," Fredda said. "Three krak."

We all agreed that was really nice.

Lily cleared her throat dramatically. "Why is it that all we ever talk about is the Prime Game?" She picked up the three krak. "Chow. Two bam."

I thought that was a little uncalled for. We had fun imagining what they were doing. Who was Lily to act like she was above it all and the rest of us were losers? No way to get popular.

We changed the topic to recipes, *Falcon Crest*, and Swatch watches, which were what everyone's grandkids were asking for.

I played like I was on fire that night. I won nine games out of the sixteen. In all my years of playing, I had never taken more than six games out of sixteen, which is considered pretty good. The first three wins felt lucky, the next four felt like skill, but the last two, those were pure attitude.

I did a good job, taking control of the women that night. I asked for umpteen favors and everyone bent over backwards to oblige. I started off small, like asking for a plate and some napkins, and ended up really big, like asking Ethel to come with me to the beauty parlor the following week. I know that doesn't sound like much of a favor but we usually went to different beauty parlors, so it was a big deal for her. I also walked out with two dinner dates and another mall-walk.

The Villa loves a winner.

I got home around eleven. I was tired, but also peppy. That happens when you're old sometimes -- your body feels conflicted. I did some quick math and realized that it was only eight o'clock in California where my son Seth lived. Since coming up with my new strategy of asking favors, I had been thinking about what I could ask of my sons. I wondered if I could build them up to an actual visit. I figured asking them point-blank to come see me would be too pathetic. Instead, I asked Seth to make me a tape of a Duke Ellington record from his collection. He was a big collector of jazz and I knew I could count on him getting excited about it. He talked my ear off for thirty minutes, until he had to go because it was Sarah's bedtime -- that's my granddaughter. I had no idea what he was talking about, comparing Duke Ellington with a bunch of other people I didn't know, but I would have listened all night.

The next morning, my phone rang at about seven. I was already on my balcony sipping orange juice. I ran inside, worried and wondering who might have died.

Greta was on the phone. She'd already heard about my big win and wanted to know my "secret." I said it was my t-shirt. She asked me to join her and Letta at the mall that morning for a walk. There must have been about ten different mall-walking groups in our complex. They all went to the same mall and pretty much walked around, looking at who was together. I accepted.

Just as I hung up the phone, it rang again. It was Lottie with an invitation for lunch at the bagel shop. I hung up and it rang again. Early-bird special with Sadie. I couldn't believe it. While I was on with Yetta, Daisy made an emergency breakthrough. When I finally hung up with Daisy, I looked at the phone for a moment, half-expecting it to ring and half-expecting to wake up from a dream. I gave it a few seconds and then headed back to the balcony. But before I got there, the phone rang.

When the calls finally stopped, I walked into my living room and spun around, laughing. I knew that popular people never behaved like that, since they were used to their phones ringing off the hook; it's only unpopular people who get excited when the phone rings. But I didn't care. I was just having too much fun. I dropped into a chair, exhausted, and then decided that dancing around wasn't such a good idea after all. If a pimple could spoil the popularity of prom queen, I could only imagine what a hip replacement would do to mine. I grabbed a napkin from the coffee table and patted some sweat from my head. What the heck, I thought, and took a big old bite out of it.

Letta's car smelled like cat. Letta smelled like cat. She always had cat hair stuck to her clothing and when I opened the car door, a puff of cat hair flew out. Letta was strange, and she rubbed some people the wrong way. When we pulled up to the parking lot, there was a kid at the ticket booth. Letta rolled down her window, leaned out, and waved a handicapped permit. Then she said real loud, "Do you honor this?" and waved the permit around like it was on fire. The kid said, "Sure we honor it, but you still have to pay for the parking." She threw the permit up on the dashboard, shook her head so that her glasses chains rattled back and forth against her head, and drove in.

There was an entrance that opened early for mall walkers and already, a small crowd had gathered outside. Letta and Greta sat on a bench to change into their Hush Puppies. I had mine on already. It was cool out, since it was so early. A man was leading a few women in stretches.

I was just standing around when Sadie, Tillie, Lottie and Marta walked up. Behind them, about fifty feet away, I could see Doris, Daisy and Sylvia.

Sadie's group came right up to me. "Hey, Minnie," Lottie said. At first, I thought that maybe they didn't see Greta and Letta on the bench behind me.

"Heard you're walking with Greta," Sadie said, pinching her lips together, her lipstick making a jagged outline of her mouth. I guess she felt slighted since I had walked with her Sunday.

"I told her to get those shoes," Sadie said, turning to Tillie and pointing at my mall walkers.

"She sure did," I said. "They're like walking on pillows." I walked around a bit to demonstrate. Sadie beamed.

Doris, Daisy and Sylvia walked up. Everyone was talking about my great night at the table. Then Doris cleared her throat. Everyone got quiet, but she didn't say anything. Sylvia's face went sour.

"I really like that one," Daisy said, pointing at my "Shopaholic" t-shirt.

I started to explain some things about it, when a security guard appeared and unlocked the doors. The guard only managed to open one door before everyone was pushing and shoving in. Greta held onto me and we got behind Letta, who crammed her way through. A woman tried to squeeze past us and got stuck against the closed door. "Serves you right," Letta said, pushing by.

It was a weird scene. I mean, it wasn't like a buffet where the food would be gone if you weren't fast enough -- the mall would be there all the same, whether you were first or last. I guess it just goes to show how competitive we were. I've watched old women nearly come to blows over who had worse rheumatism.

Once inside, we all poured down the entrance hallway, past the directory, to the first corner where World Imports, Zales, Radio Shack, and Footlocker were located. Doris and her crew took a right; Sadie's bunch went straight ahead; Greta, Letta and

I made a sharp left. There was a large island with three palm trees and a small fish pond in the center. Everything was closed.

We were walking pretty fast, with Letta setting the pace. She pumped her arms like a kid pretending to be a train, her nylon sweat suit swishing like crazy. "C'mon, girls," she said, as Greta and I fell behind.

We zoomed past Banana Republic and Wicks 'N' Sticks. Greta was a little out of breath and she and I laughed when we both sighed real loudly at the same time.

Some women approached from another direction and one of them waved to Letta, who was a store-length ahead of us already. Letta just kept chugging like a steam engine.

"Hey, there's Sylvia," I said to Greta. Syl, Doris and Daisy were walking straight at us at a pretty good pace. I thought we were on a collision course until Letta swerved and led us to an escalator. She stopped short at the bottom, staring at the moving steps for a moment. Then she hopped on. That little pause gave Greta and me a chance to catch up and the three of us glided up to the second floor together. The three of them passed underneath us. I waved and made a little dramatic wipe of my forehead. They laughed and I smiled to Greta.

"Min, have you considered playing with us on Wednesdays?" Greta said. I thought I would fall backward down the escalator. I didn't want to sound too eager, but I also knew I couldn't pretend not to care.

"Are you considering me?" I said finally, which I thought was a good answer.

"We're down to a short list. And you're on it."

I looked up at the back of Letta, who was staring out over the railing at the tops of the palm trees.

"She's as deaf as a doorknob," Greta said.

As soon as Letta reached the top, she was off like a shot. Swish, swish, swish.

Greta and I hopped off and walked a little slower, letting Letta take a real lead on us.

"What about Sylvia?" I said.

"She's on the short list, too. But..." She paused. "We may break up the game."

I stopped short. "What?" Greta gently took my arm. I took a few steps with her and then stopped short again. "What?" I said real dramatically, which I thought was a pretty good comic delivery.

Greta laughed. "Sadie and I have been talking. We're thinking about starting another game. It would be nice to play with three new women.

That just blew me away. How was it possible? The Villa had only one Prime Game.

"What about Pearl?" I asked.

"Pearl's happy with whatever. Her first love is tennis and her second love is men. Mahjongg is just something she does in between." Letta disappeared around a corner and Greta and I slowed down a little more.

I felt like shrieking with laughter. My head swirled around. I wished Frank were alive. I needed to tell someone. To tell him. "Well, I'd enjoy playing at your table. I'm sure you'll keep me posted," I said, holding back all my questions about Doris.

When we got back to the mall entrance, Letta was standing there tapping her watch at us. "One mile in twenty one minutes, thirty two seconds," she said.

"That's our time?" Greta asked.

Letta shook her head and laughed. It was her time. Ours was closer to thirty minutes. She told us that some of the other women had already finished up and gone home. She had been waiting nearly ten minutes and was about to leave us there.

Good old Letta.

The next day, I woke up at six fifteen. Lottie was having everyone over that evening. Fridays were typically reserved for early-bird specials, so it was a pretty bold move for Lottie. But by then, word had spread that there would be an announcement; Lottie was right to figure no one would miss her get-together, even for half-priced broiled chicken and rolls at the Rascal House.

An hour later, I cancelled all my appointments for the day. I did it without telling anyone why, hoping they would all think I was canceling to do something better. My plan was to practice making Ardell's brisket. Even with Greta's overtures, I figured I could lock in a place at the table with that meat.

I had a little test kitchen going, with a bunch of small briskets ready to go into the oven. By eleven o'clock, I was sure I'd hit the mark. I carefully noted the amount of grape jelly on my own recipe card, and got busy making a big brisket for the party.

Lottie's apartment was already packed when I arrived. The buffet table was crowded with at least three other briskets, four string bean casseroles, three moulds, two trays of Saucy Susan chicken with noodles, three angel food Jell-O cakes, and hundreds of cookies. It was more like a banquet than a buffet. I couldn't find a place to put mine down. I asked Tillie if she would make a little room for my brisket on the table. She obliged immediately.

I was wearing my Lucky Lady shirt, pink, with big bubble letters on it and pieces of felt arranged in the shape of a flower. Everyone complimented me on it. It was like walking down the red carpet at the Academy Awards. Everyone turned to say hello and see what I was wearing, and then they all turned back as I passed and I could hear them whispering about me. "Nine games," I heard someone say. "She's a shoo-in." I glowed.

I stood next to Sylvia, who pretended not to see me. I wasn't going to play that game with her and I said hello. "Oh, hiya, Minnie," she said. "I see you brought a brisket, huh? Wait 'til you taste mine. You're not going to believe it."

"Well, you better just save some room for mine," I said. She looked at me funny for a second. But she said nothing and went to find another conversation. So I started to work the room. I talked to four women for a while about *Falcon Crest*, then to another group about *Wheel of Fortune*. Apparently, Daisy had invited Pearl and Greta over to watch *Wheel* the previous night and she had guessed each puzzle before any letters were up. It turned out that Daisy had taped the show on her Betamax a few days before, and then played the tape, pretending it was the real thing. They caught her because there was a clip about that reporter Jessica Savitch being incoherent in a broadcast, which had happened days before. Daisy tried to play it cool, saying it was all a big joke. Pearl and Greta played along. They were too nice to call her on it. They even repeated the story, saying that Daisy put one over on them. But we all knew that Daisy was trying to look smart.

Suddenly, the room got quiet. The foursome had arrived. Sylvia started talking really loud. I missed the first bit because everyone started to shush her. But when she said something about Ardell, everyone got quiet.

"I have a little announcement to make." Sylvia raised her hands up like a champion. "I know the secret to Ardell's brisket!" Everyone started to talk and Sylvia looked around nodding at everyone. I was stunned. Sylvia was going to steal my show.

"Yes, it's true," Sylvia said and everyone got quiet again. "Ardell wrote to me. She sent me a letter with the recipe before she died and it came yesterday." She produced the paper and waved it around.

My heart sank and my hands went numb. I felt faint. Ardell. You bitch. She was picking Sylvia from beyond the grave. There was no way they would pick me now for the Prime Game. You can't argue with a dead woman. It was going to be Sylvia -- ordained by the spirit of Ardell.

"So, what's the secret?" Daisy brayed.

Sylvia smiled real smug and wagged her finger.

The women started arguing with her, and it got really loud again. They kept saying, "come on" and "tell us."

"It's Smucker's grape jelly," I yelled.

Sylvia's face turned pale. She looked at me as if I had just run over her dog. I instantly felt very stupid and ugly -- mostly ugly.

People looked like they were waiting for me to say something. "That's not it," someone said. "It's got to be thyme."

Everyone kept looking at me. I wished they would turn back to Sylvia. If only Ardell had lived long enough for me to ask her some favors. She would have picked me.

"She's right," Sylvia said, in a voice that almost sounded ashamed. "It's Smucker's grape jelly."

There was a pause. Silence. Dangling earrings pinged softly like wind chimes on a porch. There was a kind of low rumbling that sounded like a hundred women's stomachs growling at once. Then suddenly, there was an abrupt rush to the buffet. Our briskets -- Sylvia's and mine -- were gone in a matter of seconds. The words "grape jelly" echoed through the room. The women set out to judge whose brisket was closer to Ardell's. It was a bitter-sweet victory to hear that mine won, even if I wasn't hand picked by Ardell. I tried to convince people otherwise, but it didn't matter. Sylvia walked away from me each time I approached her. I didn't blame her.

Then Doris coughed loudly.

In the excitement over the briskets, people had forgotten that there would be news about the Prime Game.

When she absolutely had everyone's attention, Doris said, "I think Sylvia's is better." I caught Greta and Sadie look at each other with surprise. I figured Doris wasn't following whatever plan they had discussed. But it didn't matter; the damage was done. Sylvia screeched, threw her arms out, and then hugged someone near her. Greta, Pearl and Sadie probably would have agreed that Ardell's chosen one should play with them, but I still think they wanted a say.

I snuck out shortly after the announcement. Sylvia came over and sort-of allowed me to congratulate her. No one was really paying any attention to me anymore and I felt completely alone in the crowd.

My walk home was pretty dismal. It was humid out and I was sweating like crazy. I knew I would be cold as soon as I walked into my apartment because I had left the air-conditioner on, just in case someone came back with me to celebrate.

I was right, of course, my place was freezing. I felt clammy and sticky at the same time. It was disgusting. I thought about taking a shower but was too sad to muster the energy. I just sat in my chair for a while, like a heavy lump of brisket.

I looked over at the answering machine, which was blinking. I laughed. About an hour ago, I was in; now I was out, just like that. Actually, I felt lower than when I'd started. I wished I had never gotten popular. I guess I was pretty happy being unpopular. Well, maybe not happy, but at least I hadn't been a jerk.

On my way to bed, I hit the play button on the answering machine. I didn't want to hear the invitations that were left before I was the unpopular me again, I just wanted the stupid machine to stop blinking.

I slunk a few paces down the hallway, then I whirled around when I heard my son Seth's voice.

"Hi, mom. Just wanted you to know I sent the tape this morning. Hey, also, I'd like to come to see you in three weeks if that's okay. We were planning to go to skiing, but, well, it's been a while. Call me when you can and let me know if that works."

I shot my fist into the air and let out a big "yahoo!" The funniest part is, I actually thought about telling him I was busy in three weeks. But of course, I forgot that plan as soon as I came to my senses.

***

Birdie P., December 14, 1983; Letta D., December 6, 1984; Fredda M., January 2, 1986; Daisy T. March 5, 1989; Marta M., May 27, 1989; Sylvia A., September 19, 1991; Doris R., February 4, 1992; Sadie V., September 12, 1993; Gloria S., April 15, 1994; Lily C., April 27, 1994; Gladys L., May 15, 1996; Ethel P., January 5, 1997; Lottie S., February 5, 1997; Tillie S., October 31, 1998; Pearl B., May 23, 2001

It may have felt like time was flowing in circles around Wednesdays, but of course that's not what was happening.

I miss the old gang. Greta and I are the only ones left. She moved closer to her son, who lives in Tampa. We talk now and then, but not often. My sons are retired and living in Scottsdale and San Diego. I told them my secret favor-asking strategy a long time ago, when they started complaining that their kids don't come to see them often enough. We have a good laugh about that from time to time.

There's no Prime Game anymore. There's no game at all, actually. Ever since the casinos opened up, the women of Villa Puesta Del Sol stopped socializing. We chat when we pass each other in the hallways, about who won, who lost, and how much. We complain about the casino staff.

I spend three nights a week at the casino. I have a nifty casino t-shirt with a slot machine on it with rhinestone cherries. I won a hundred and fifty dollars last week in this shirt.

I look around the casino before I push the button to give the slots a spin. An old man with a cane and a woman with silver hair are shuffling slowly toward a machine. She's holding his arm in one hand and a bucket of change in the other. They look sad.

One of the many not-so-funny things about getting old is that you become an expert in doctors' waiting rooms. I once heard someone refer to Florida as God's waiting room, which made me think of the Villa as our own private section in it. It strikes me that there won't be any waiting rooms like that one anymore, where you made food, got together, played, talked and tried to be someone you weren't in high school.

It's sad, this new waiting room. It's filled with slot machines, people who don't talk except to order drinks, and waitresses in short skirts who call you "dear" but don't really mean it.

WHAT'S UP, KIKE?

J osh Ellis leaned back and rested his head against the cool wall of the subway car. Having lived in Manhattan for five years now, he had learned to block out the ongoing clamor of his morning commute, transforming the panhandlers' pleas, door chimes and recorded station announcements into a steady flow of white noise beneath New York's streets.

But at the moment, he could not ignore the woman sitting opposite him. He had noticed recently that the subway had become another arena in the Upper East Side battle of maternal one-upmanship. It seemed every mother had something to prove. Take this woman. He had seen a lot of women reading to their kids with big, bellowing voices on the subway as they accompanied them to school — looking around every so often to see who was watching. But this one...

"Collisionless plasma. KA Blaaaaam!"

"Maxwellian ground state. Wooooosh!"

Josh opened his eyes and saw that the woman was shaking her head like a rabid dog tearing at a bone.

Her daughter: five, maybe six.

"Coherent radiation from blazer jets. RrrrruuusssH!"

Her reading selection: *Astronomy and Astrophysics Review*, which is, of course, rocket science.

Mothers.

He closed his eyes again. His heart beat quicker and he clasped his hands tightly in his lap. Suddenly he was thinking about his wife. Sarah would probably be a *Wall-Street-Journal*-reading mother, he thought, if they had a kid.

There had been another argument last night about starting a family. It was the latest in a fight that began several months back -- on Valentine's Day to be precise. That's when Sarah had let it slip that she was no longer on birth control, claiming that her doctor had said she was retaining a dangerous amount of water. She had just forgotten to tell Josh that she was off the pill.

Oops.

Since then, their sex life had taken a nosedive. Last night, irritated by Sarah's eagerness to "make a baby," Josh informed her that he had been wearing tight underwear, bicycling at the gym and spending time in the sauna after workouts to lower his sperm count. Sarah threw a biological clock at Josh, however premature, and Josh body slammed her with the forecasted cost of tuition.

They had been married for about two years and in two more, they would both be thirty years old.

The horror.

Friends and family continually asked when children were coming, which wore on them differently. Sarah thought it was a veiled warning, like when a parent says to a teenager, "Are you getting a job or do you intend to go the entire summer with no money?"

Josh was just irritated by the sheer invasion of privacy. A friend of Sarah's recently cornered him at a party and asked why he wasn't giving Sarah a baby. He looked quickly behind him, lowered his voice, then said that what Sarah hadn't confided in *this* friend was that she had some kind of ovarian dysfunction -- producing too much mucus -- and that Josh's sperm had blood in it. Then he went into a long, concocted story about freezing sperm, surrogate mothers and adoption. "We're completely devastated," he said in conclusion to her now pale and unmoving face. "And with you, nu?"

He remembered a time before they were married when Sarah had played along with him, discussing a life of travel with no roots, the whole of their lives fitting into two backpacks and a carry-on. But less than two months into the marriage, Sarah's alternate plans started to pop up, forcing Josh to muster whatever defense he could to whack them back down. Car. Whack. House in Connecticut. Whack. Passover with the in-laws. Whack. Kids. Whack. Whack. Whack.

"Non-thermal radiation! Yaaaay!"

Grrr...

"What's up, kike?"

Josh's eyes flew open. He must have been mistaken. He couldn't have heard that.

He looked around the subway car. Two boys were standing near the doors. Both were about fifteen years old, wearing knit yarmulkes, jeans and large sweatshirts.

Who would say such a thing to them? Others on the subway had their heads buried in newspapers or books. Some were zoning out on their headphones. How could this happen? This is New York, dammit. No one talks like that unless he plans to run for mayor.

Then he saw the boys clasp hands, pull toward one another and give each other a tender shoulder bump.

"Not much, kike," one said.

"Whoa!" thought Josh. Wait. He just... Cool. He felt a sudden urge to give a speech or, lacking a podium, find a fight. He sat up a little straighter.

His mind flew back to when he was sixteen, playing a video game at the corner candy store with two friends. Out of nowhere, something had smacked him on the head, leaving a sharp sting on his temple before plunking down onto the game screen. It was a penny. He glanced at his friends, who were staring straight ahead. Several boys were behind them, pushing them around a bit.

One of the kids, blond hair, an attempt of a beard sprouting from his chin, threw another penny at Josh, hitting him in the shoulder. "Hey, kike, you need another penny?" he said.

Josh had no idea how the bullies knew he and his friends were Jewish. His two friends practically looked like models for the Dutch Boy paint logo. Josh himself was often mistaken for being a gentile. "I wonder," a girlfriend's mother would sometimes start, "What kind of name is Ellis?" It was changed from Ilyenko -- Russian for Elijah -- he would explain. "It was a tenement thing."

One of the bullies pushed it further. "Hey kike, here's another penny for the machine," and then threw another coin. Josh turned to the boys and said, "The machine takes quarters." Before any of the kids had a chance to respond, Josh showed them that a full roll of quarters to the face did a lot more damage than a penny.

Back in the subway car, the taboo word swirled in Josh's mind.

"What's up, kike?" he said to himself. It was a statement of strength. This must be what black kids felt when they call each other "nigga." It was ownership. And "kike" not only stung with its vulgarity, it also had the added benefit of bookend Ks -- an acoustical slap in the face that has the connotation of physical harm, like the words "battering ram," "blitzkrieg" or "colonoscopy."

"Thermal equilibrium… Yahooooooo!"

Watching the two boys step off the train, Josh briefly considered whether misspelling "kike" would give it that street-side, fuck-the-system coolness of "niggaz." No way. "Kike" could be misspelled with diacritics (kĭk or kīx), which made it look more like a brand of Czech dishwashing soap than a word that would make someone cross to the other side of the street. Besides, everyone knows the fuck-you-we're-smart thing never turns out well for the Jews.

About fifteen minutes later, Josh entered his office building and waited in the lobby for an elevator to bring him to the eleventh floor, where the firm of Laskey, Askey and Feinberg was located. "Three kikes," he laughed to himself, looking at the building directory. He still felt the fire of the word in him as he entered the elevator. Just as the door was closing, he saw Mike Rosen sprinting towards him. Normally, Josh would pretend not to see him and let the elevator shut, but he jabbed the button to open the door and his colleague hustled inside. Mike nodded in thanks, then turned to face the shutting doors and looked up at the display of floor numbers.

"No sweat, kike," Josh said to the back of his colleague's head.

Mike turned around slowly. "What did you just say, Ellis?"

"I said," Josh hesitated, "no sweat, Mike." He tugged gingerly at his collar. "What did you think I said?"

"Never mind."

They reached the floor and went their separate ways. Josh got to his office, threw his briefcase on his desk and plopped down in his seat.

His first experiment was a complete failure and he slouched a bit. Rosen should have joined the movement without hesitation. He was one of the kikiest kikes Josh knew. Josh once saw Rosen rip into a defendant's attorney when the man referred to Rosen's client, whose last name was Rosenberg, as "shrewd." "I suspect he's clever and sly as well?" Rosen had said. "Maybe he's even a bit cunning, having taken on his *human look*. That's what Hitler said, right?" The case was settled very much in favor of Mr. Rosenberg about forty minutes later.

It must have been his delivery, Josh thought. After all, he had said "kike" so meekly, so offhandedly, that he had easily convinced Rosen that it was a misunderstanding. He needed to brandish the word like a gun, with conviction.

Eric Stern ducked into Josh's office to ask him if he wanted anything from the coffee shop in the lobby. Eric was the perfect subject; he was more friend than colleague and he thought himself to be "street," despite the fact that he shopped in the portly section of discount men's suit shops and his shirts never stayed fully tucked into his pants. To Eric, everyone was "dude" or "man." He grew up in the Bronx, which gave him an excuse to hint about a tough childhood. In truth, he'd grown up in the Riverdale area. That's the tony section where stone mansions sit behind sycamore-lined streets and well manicured lawns. But it's still da Bronx. In fact, Eric would always mention the Bronx before he would mention he went to Harvard. It gave him just a touch more swagger than the other Harvard lawyers who littered the office.

"You want any va?" Eric asked. "Java" was so passé.

Josh stood up and walked toward his friend with as much of a strut as he could muster. He was a full head taller than Eric. He glared down at his colleague, gave him a quick head flick, and swung his right arm around in a slow, large arc, choreographed to give Eric time to react.

At first, Eric gave Josh a look with narrowed eyes and a slightly cocked head -- the kind of look usually reserved for approaching beggars. But then he caught on, reaching out to grab Josh's hand. Their palms met with a loud, satisfying clap and they weaved their thumbs together. Then they pulled their hands apart, leaving a crisp snap hanging in the air. Josh looked at Eric dead in the face.

"No, I'm good, my kike." He hit the double *K*s hard to ensure there was no mistake and leaned into Eric's shoulder to give it a bump. "How was the weekend?"

"Did you just call me a kike, Ellis?"

"What, a kike can't call his kike a kike?"

Eric took a step back and stared at Josh for a moment. "Okay," he said wryly. "I'll play. Why are you calling me a kike, Ellis?"

Josh took a deep breath. "Awww, man. If we ain't the kikes like the blacks are the n—"

"Aye!" Eric said, covering Josh's mouth with his hands. He quickly shut the door behind him, peering out through the crack as it closed to see if anyone had been listening.

Josh threw his hands up. "Say what, kike? This place is full of kikes."

"'Say what?' Before I even begin to indulge you in this conversation, Ellis, drop the *Good Times* crap. You sound like an idiot." Josh started to speak, but Eric shushed him. "Have you lost your mind, Ellis? If Feinberg heard you say that, or better, if

Tanya heard you say that? Imagine if the only black woman in this white bread law firm heard some stupid punk Jew say that word."

"Kike? Why would she care?"

"Not that. The other word. You know..." Eric said, and jerked his head to the side several times, grunting with each shake.

"Okay, fine, but what makes you think Feinberg and the rest of them wouldn't call themselves kikes? These guys are like the Bugsy Siegels of the bar association."

Eric opened the door. "You mean like Krantz?" He pointed at a man with thin, scattered remnants of grey hair, who was holding several manila folders and walking across the rug as if he were stepping through a shallow puddle. "Krantz eats ham with mayonnaise. Krantz hasn't been to temple since Feinberg's daughter had her bat mitzvah ten years ago. Krantz owns a Mercedes."

"Yeah, but I bet if you pushed him, he'd fight back," Josh said just as Krantz dropped his folders. They splattered across the floor. Krantz threw his hands up, pointed to Tanya to take care of them, and walked off. "What the hell's gotten into you today?" Eric squeezed Josh's shoulder. "Was it the women reading to their kids on the subway again?" he asked with exaggerated concern.

Josh wished he had never mentioned that to Eric. Everything Josh said in the office could be -- and was -- used against him at some point.

Lawyers.

There were many things Josh wanted to say to defend himself, but the rebuttals refused to line up. "Fuck you," he finally offered.

"Right," Eric said. "Latte?"

Later that morning, Sarah called to apologize for the fight. Actually, what she said was that she was sorry the fight occurred. All of their confrontations ended this way, as if they had accidentally stepped into a pile of crap. Nobody was to blame; it was just an unfortunate event. Sarah told Josh that their friends the Lowensteins had invited them over for dinner, which he could have predicted. It had become a ritual to see Jill and Mark Lowenstein following a fight about having kids.

"So we're good with last night and for Jill and Mark's, right?" Sarah said, steering the conversation to a close.

No, he was not good with any of it. She had lied to him about birth control. Not directly, but by omission. On top of which, he had free-floating hatred of the Lowensteins, who always asked their Guyanese cook to make something unrecognizable as food when Sarah and Josh were over, thanks to Sarah's gushing about their staff's cooking. Josh usually got through the night by playing a silent drinking game -- taking a swig each time someone said "ethnic." He always ended up sloshed. God he hated pau pau and that stinky rice thing with the fish heads. At the previous dinner, Josh had suddenly realized that the word "delicacy" was just a euphemism for the disgusting parts of animals. No one ever calls a sixty-dollar flank steak a delicacy, but a duck's ass, now that's something special. The thought of Mark's fat face plowing through a plate of that slop made him want to vomit.

"Why the hell not," Josh responded. "I haven't seen those kikes in a while."

There was a long pause.

"I said--" Josh started.

"I heard what you said, Josh. I can't even begin--"

"What? I haven't seen them in a long time. What a month?"

"Josh, you know what I mean. If you don't want to see them, just say so. Calling them names is just childish. Actually, I'm hanging up."

"No. Don't go. Okay, you're right. I don't want to see them. But that has nothing to do with the fact that they're kikes."

"Goodbye."

"Wait, listen; Eric and I decided to take the word back."

"I should have known. Tell Eric to grow up."

"It's not like that."

"Whatever. Are we going tonight?" Sarah said.

"Sure."

"We can meet in their lobby at seven. See you later, then."

"See you later, then, what?"

"Josh, don't be an idiot."

"Bye, kikela," Josh sang into the phone.

"Now you're calling me a kike?"

"Well, more like my little kike."

He thought he heard the slightest hint of a laugh before she slammed the phone down.

Eric walked in.

"Sarah sends her regards to her second most favorite kike," Josh said.

Eric rolled his eyes and started to talk about a complaint he was filing. It was a complicated explanation and Josh tried to listen, but he had just plugged "kike" into his search engine. Josh turned his computer screen around to face Eric. "Shit," Eric said quietly.

Nearly every hit was steaming with fanatical hatred. The abstracts beneath each link stoked the smoldering embers of their fears to a healthy orange glow. "Too many Kikes and Nigs," "Dirty Kikes," "Russian Kikes," "Commie Kikes," "Gay Kikes," "The Kike Jew Mafia," "The Kikes did 9/11."

Josh breathed loudly. "Is there a word for when you're surprised, but not really surprised? I mean, I can't believe this shit, but yet, I sort-of can, right?"

"Crazy," Eric said. "Well, anyway, would love to stay and play, but I have to get this done and then prepare for the Monthly."

"Aw shit. The monthly meeting's today?" He pulled up his calendar. "At two? Dammit. Stupid kikes."

"Hundred bucks says you won't say kike in the meeting."

Josh curled his lip and held Eric's gaze. "Double or nothing I get Feinberg to say it."

"You mean Max, right? Not Molly."

"Yep. Max. Head of the firm. Super-kike."

Eric blew a laugh at Josh. "Oh, definitely. But you can't bribe him to say it and it doesn't count if he says something like, 'Did you just say, 'kike,' Ellis? You're fired."

They shook on it.

About two and a half hours into the monthly meeting, most of the attendees were at least forty minutes into a light siesta. Josh was having a hard time keeping his head from dropping and he slouched down to better rest his head against the back of the chair.

His phone vibrated.

He dug it from his pocket and held it up to his face, staring at the text message with one eye closed. "Let's go, kike," the message said. He opened his other eye and looked beyond his phone at Eric, who was tapping his pen against a yellow legal pad and smirking in the direction of the head partners. The partners were deep into their recurring deliberation concerning the status of the firm's casual Friday policy. The old men had their heads buried in the employee handbook and were debating the wording of the dress code.

All of the partners were in favor of ending the business casual policy, particularly Feinberg. The whole issue would have been easily resolved if the six men had simply taken a vote. But there was a small problem standing in their way -- a problem named Molly Feinberg.

Molly was the head of human resources. More importantly, she was the daughter of Max Feinberg; and despite her relegation to back-office paperwork concerning new hires, benefits and exit interviews, she had somehow seized veto power over the firm's dress code. The partners had been afraid of losing productive attorneys and Molly had convinced them that a happy work environment was a productive work environment, and for some reason, this hinged on collared shirts and khaki pants.

H.R.

Josh perked up and surveyed the room. Of the twenty people present, eighteen were Jews, including the firm's six partners. He looked at Eric, whose grin widened when he glanced at his watch.

"My grandfather," Josh began, bringing the room to an immediate and complete silence. It was, in fact, the first interruption in the long history of the monthly meetings. Not that speaking up was discouraged; it was just that no one did it. Aside from the partners and Molly, the rest of the participants viewed the meetings as a sanctioned rest period -- adult nap time.

Josh cleared his throat. "My grandfather was a tailor. He came to New York around nineteen hundred and six from Russia." Krantz and Lepinski looked at each other. Josh knew they were Russian -- second generation Americans. It was touted on the firm's website. The remaining partners were either Russian, German, or half-breed New York mutts.

Josh continued. "He, my grandfather that is, worked as a suit tailor in a little shop on Essex, down on the Lower East Side." The partners all seemed to brighten up at this. "He met my grandmother there, in the sewing room. She was a seamstress. Well, anyway, I know this is a long story. But what I wanted to say was that he dealt with a lot of stuff as an immigrant. They called him names like kike and…"

Krantz slapped his hand on the table, drawing all attention to him. He looked sternly at Josh, furrowing his white, thick eyebrows. "Kike?" he said sternly.

"I'm sor--"

Krantz cut him off. "Shuddup. They didn't call him kike, Ellis. That's anachronistic. The Germans brought that word over later during the forties. They would have called him a *sheeney*."

"No, they'd have called him an *Ikey Mo*," Lasky added. "That's what they called my dad."

"Ikey Mo," Feinberg said. "I haven't heard that one in ages. That was a good one. But you're wrong, Krantz, they said kike back then. We even used the word. My father told me that he thought that *kolpiks* were actually called kikes until he was about nine because whenever my grandfather saw a *chassid* wearing one of those big furry hats, he would mumble 'kike' under his breadth."

Josh managed to keep back his smile when Eric smacked his own forehead.

Josh told the partners about the two boys on the train. He walked over to Feinberg and said, "Here, stand up. It was like this." And he grabbed his hand, pulled him close and said, "What's up, kike?"

Fienberg laughed. "What's up, Kike? Just like that?"

"Exactly," Josh said.

"Um, excuse me," Molly said. "But that's enough. I don't know what this has to do with anything office-related."

"Hey, sheeney," Krantz said to Lasky, waving across the table.

"Hello, ikey mo!" Lasky gleefully waved back.

"My mother and father," intoned Feinberg, looking at Molly to remind her that he was the boss, and was about to talk about her grandparents, "also started out on the Lower East Side, Josh. They worked themselves ragged putting me through school."

"There is no greater love than that of a parent sacrificing for a child," Tanya said from the corner. "I hope you all experience that love one day."

Yeah, right, thought Josh. The old guy was talking about a time when college cost two chickens and a cup of coffee. And the kids worked at school! He wasn't going to get himself into hundreds of thousands of dollars in debt so his kid could skip class, get stoned and spend weeks in multi-level videogame tournaments.

Molly smiled. This was exactly the kind of breakthrough she had been hoping for. In terms of keeping associates from quitting, her father's brief disclosure about her grandparents was worth millions in bonus money. Employees love to be a part of an organization with a soul. She turned to Josh with a motherly look upon her face. Had she been sitting closer, he was sure that she would have clasped his hand in hers. "What were you going to say about your grandfather, Josh?"

Josh tried to remember what his point was going to be. There had been no point to the story. He was really just looking for an excuse to slip "kike" in during the meeting. Now everyone was looking at him.

"Ahem," he said, buying a precious few seconds to collect his thoughts. "Well, the point was that my grandfather, who, as I said, worked as a tailor down on Essex Street on the Lower East Side. He... uh, well, he never had casual Fridays. In fact, he used to get dressed up to go to the theatre or the library or just to walk around on a Sunday. He hated when people looked shabby. He had a really great work ethic and in fact, dressing up was a part of it. You know, he was a kike--"

"Stop that," Molly said. The partners laughed.

"Okay, he was a, what was it, a sheeney?" The partners burst out laughing. "He worked really hard and putting on a tie was part of that feeling of empowerment. I, for one, would have no problem wearing a tie every day. I think looking smart is better for morale than dressing down."

Molly tried to launch a counterargument, but the damage was done. Business casual at Lasky, Askey and Feinberg had been crumpled up and tossed into the wastebasket.

Eric came to Josh's office after the meeting, agreeing that he lost the hundred when Josh had said kike the first time, but that Josh lost the double or nothing bet since Fienberg only said kike, he didn't call someone kike. "What's up? Kike? Just like that?" Eric imitated, sounding more like a Borscht Belt caricature than Feinberg. Before Josh could respond, Eric slapped two hundred dollars onto Josh's desk.

"Mazel tov, Ellis. You can buy yourself a two hundred dollar tie to wear on Fridays from now on, ya dumb-ass kike, ya."

Josh invited Eric out for a drink to celebrate his victory. He had about an hour to kill before heading over to the Lowensteins. They sat side-by-side on the high stools in front of the bar and ordered.

"I told you they'd go for it," Josh said.

"Yeah, yeah."

"I'm telling you, this is something we can start. We can take back the word."

"No one is using the word, Josh. There's nothing to take back."

They went back and forth for a while, and just as they ordered a second drink, someone leaned over to place an order and bumped into Josh.

Josh pushed back against the man.

"Excuse you," the man said.

"What?" Josh said standing.

"I said--"

"Did you just call me a kike?"

Eric slowly shook his head. The man, who a moment ago had puffed his chest when Josh had purposefully bumped him, deflated as soon as he heard the word. The change in posture was instantaneous, like he was a kid caught with a book of matches that suddenly went behind his back.

"No, I didn't call you that."

"Yeah, bitch. I heard you say it. You called me a kike."

A few people nearby leaned in to eavesdrop.

"Look," the man said to Josh. "You see this guy coming over here? That's my buddy." He pointed to a muscular bald man with a goatee, who was walking toward them. "He's a Jew."

"Oh, so some of your best friends are Jews?"

"I don't mean it like that. Look there's obviously a misunderstanding; I just want to get a drink. Let me buy you one."

"Now I'm too cheap to buy one myself?"

"What's going on?" the bald man asked when he stepped up.

"Misunderstanding," the friend said.

"This guy says you're a kike," Josh said.

The man hit Josh so fast that he thought someone had pulled him from behind and thrown him to the floor.

Josh stood at the Lowensteins' apartment door with a dirty bar rag pressed against his eye. Sarah had gone up when he had not shown up exactly at seven. He looked at his face in the hallway mirror. There wasn't much swelling, just a small cut below his eye with a dark, moody bruise forming around it.

He knocked on the door. Aaron, the Lowenstein's six-year-old, opened the door. His four-year-old sister Amy appeared behind him.

"Mom!" the kid yelled. "Josh's here!"

"Hi, Aaron. Hi, Amy," Josh said and asked Aaron about school.

Aaron tilted his head up to Josh. "And he got his ass kicked!" he screamed.

Brats.

"I see they cut your Ritalin dose again," Josh mumbled to himself.

Sarah came to the door. She threw her arms around him in a display of affection that caused him to lose his balance and bump the corner of a large, framed landscape that hung in the vestibule. He quickly adjusted the painting as the Lowensteins approached.

"Whoohooo," Mark Lowenstein said, with a large smile and a slap on Josh's back. "Look at that shiner. You're in for it tonight."

Joshed leaned over Sarah, kissed Jill Lowenstein and then shook hands with Mark. "One more word about it, Mark, and I tell A-A-R-O-N he's wearing shoes that were made for G-I-R-L-S."

Mark immediately lost his smile.

Jill and Sarah each took one of Josh's arms and guided him into the apartment, even though he was capable of walking on his own. They helped him sit down. Jill hustled to the kitchen.

"Don't bleed on the couch, Ellis. It's new," Mark said.

Josh took the compress off his face and turned to look into the mirror behind the sofa. He touched his eye gently and winced at the pain. His nose felt as though it were stuffed with cotton. He had a deposition downtown at ten the next morning and was sure the other attorney was going to get a kick out of

Josh showing up in a pair of sunglasses. Maybe the swelling would be gone by then.

Jill returned with a glass of water and a plastic bag full of ice.

"Honey, what happened?" Sarah said.

Josh pressed the icepack to his face and said he bumped into a door.

"Hey, babe," Mark said to Jill, "maybe you want to bring your puppets out here so Josh can tell us his story." He turned and winked at Josh.

Last year, Jill had earned a certificate in finger-puppet therapy and Mark had set her up with a practice. It was originally called, "Finger Moods." A tool and his money are soon parted, Mark had quipped when he first told Josh about it. It did so well in the first three months that they decided to bring on several other experimental psychotherapeutic practitioners: therapists in art, music, and drama, pet therapists and so on. They changed the group's name to "Leading Hearts," paid a college kid to put together a business plan, and sold the concept for national expansion.

Sarah asked if there was a steak in the freezer for Josh's eye. Jill nodded quickly and stood up.

Mark grabbed his wife's arm and pulled her back down. "Okay, that's just an old wives tale," he said, laughing nervously. "Steaks are no good for the eyes. Stick with the ice." He opened his eyes wide at Jill to give her some kind of sign.

Jill laughed off his discomfort, playfully releasing herself from his grip. She headed for the kitchen. "Come on, hon," Mark pleaded. "They're Kobe. They cost fifty bucks a piece. Ellis, get my back here, huh?"

Josh said he would stick with the ice, since the thought of putting the dead flesh to his face was actually more repulsive than sticking one to Mark.

"Aaron, that's not nice," Jill said loudly, catching Aaron poking his sister with a plastic straw.

"Clara!"

The Lowensteins' nanny instantly emerged from the kitchen. Assessing the situation, she set the kids up with a puzzle at the far end of the living room.

Sarah stroked Josh's face. "Oh, baby. What did they do to you?" It was a gentle touch, but he winced every time she applied pressure.

Sarah's face suddenly tightened. From her knitted eyebrows, Josh could tell that she had just conjured up a story in her mind that involved another woman.

"It's not what you're thinking." Josh reached for her hands, just in case she had an impulse to jab him in the eye. "I was sitting in the bar by the office with Eric. We were talking about a case. This guy, blond hair, blue eyes, bumped into me. I turned around and asked if there was a problem. Not like, 'hey, you got a problem?' More like, 'excuse me, is there a problem?' Then, out of nowhere, the guy called me a..." He looked over at the kids and lowered his voice. "K-I-K-E."

"So you hit him in the fist with your face," Mark said. "Sweet."

Sarah exhaled loudly. "Are you sure that's how it happened?"

"Yeah, Josh, you're not like the hymie poster-boy," Mark added.

"I don't know, maybe he just calls everyone that. What do I know? So we had a fight. That's it."

"What an amazing coincidence." Sarah took a gulp of her wine. "Just today, you and Eric decide to start calling each other K-I-K-E-S and then some random guy in a bar, in midtown Manhattan, where a troop of Jewish lawyers hang out every day, happens to call you that out of the blue."

"I think it's a gang of lawyers," said Mark. "Troop of gorillas, gang of lawyers." He caught a flash of anger in Sarah's piercing gaze and suddenly developed a keen interest in a baby carrot, resting on a platter of crudités on their marble coffee table.

Jill turned to the housekeeper, who was still playing with the children. "Clara, is dinner ready?" Clara shrugged and went back to the kids' puzzle. Jill rolled her eyes at Sarah, then called out to the kitchen. "Marta, is dinner ready?" A thin black woman appeared at the door wearing a colorful African print dress under a white apron. She was wringing her hands. "Been ready for ten minutes."

Jill slapped her hands on her knees and stood up. "Alrighty, then. Let's head to the table. It would have been nice if someone told us it was ready, but here we go. Clara, the kids."

Clara stood up and took Aaron and Amy by the hand. The two of them went stiff, threw their heads back and let out a wail. "I want to stay!" Aaron cried. Amy broke free from Clara's light grip and ran to Sarah, wrapping her arms around her legs.

Jill gave her a stern look, and Amy clung tighter. Jill turned to Clara, who again just shrugged. "Clara," Jill said, "throw dolly bear in the trash, please."

"No!" Amy screamed.

"Then go inside."

"I don't want to," she whimpered to Sarah.

"Clara, dolly bear, trash, now."

Amy gave one last look up at Sarah, who stroked her face. "Listen to your mommy, honey."

Amy sniffled bravely, wiped her nose and walked hand-in-hand with Clara.

"They're such angels," Jill said, as the adults took their seats. Then she described the meal they were about to consume in great detail. Sarah emitted such a stream of admiration over Jill's wondercrap that Josh was actually embarrassed. The meal had some unpronounceable name, but as far as he could tell, it was basically fried chunks of beef on a scoop of Rice-A-Roni. According to Jill, Rice-A-Roni was as big in Africa as it was in San Francisco, it was just more ethnic there.

"I had Marta add a little saffron to the dish," Jill said, gently tapping two manicured fingernails on Sarah's wrist for emphasis. "Not that they have saffron in Africa." She looked straight into Sarah's eyes. "Pound for pound, saffron costs more than gold." She nodded deeply and slowly, tucking her chin in tight and sucking in her lips.

"Really?" said Sarah, outwardly touched that Jill would go to such an expense for her.

"So do Sea-Monkeys," said Josh, reaching across the table for a bottle of cola.

"Josh!" said Sarah.

Aaron came out of the kitchen. "I want soda," he said, seeing Josh's hand around the bottle.

"Oh, I'm gonna have to take that," Jill said. "It's bad for the kids. Clara shouldn't have brought it out when she set the table."

Josh looked at the bottle and then at Clara, who was busy chasing Aaron around the table. With one motion, she hoisted Aaron up onto her hip with one hand and snatched the bottle off the table with the other, then retreated to the kitchen with both. Then Amy came scurrying in and ran under the table.

With the soda bottle safely hidden and Aaron presumably secured, Clara returned to deal with Amy. Clara looked at Jill, who raised her eyebrows as if daring her to say something. Clara pulled the girl out from beneath the table, and trotted her back into the kitchen. She kicked the door jam out from the door, which started to creak closed. Josh could see her trying to stick Amy into a highchair, which was like watching someone try to thread a needle with a squid.

"Clara," Jill said, as she scooped some rice onto Sarah's plate. "Don't hold her like that."

"But how..." Clara started, as the door finally shut.

Josh tried to catch Sarah's eye, but she was too busy grinning at Jill and loudly complimenting her on Marta's meal that had somehow all appeared amidst the commotion.

No one heard Josh's exhale over the screams coming from the kitchen. He wished he could fast forward the evening to the cab ride home, when he would remind Sarah that the Lowensteins' philosophy, that "a child's life should fit into its parents' life, not the other way around," was a big joke. Even with Mark's eight-figure income and a staff that was paid to cut the crusts off sandwiches, the Lowenstein residence was hardly a paradise.

Jill placed a dollop of beef and Rice-A-Roni onto Mark's plate. The heap of food released a short puff of steam.

"Do you know what I think your problem is, Josh?" she said suddenly. Even the kitchen noise ceased. Josh looked at Mark, who shrugged.

"Your problem is that you regress when you're confronted with responsibility," Jill said. She handed Mark's plate back to him and started to dole out her own meal. "Doesn't this smell fantastic."

Puppet therapists.

Josh rolled his lips a few times and poked at his food. He cleared his throat. "That's it? I regress? Okay. I'll buy that. But really? You can't come up with something more insightful than that?"

"Josh?" Sarah said, with a begging look.

Josh forced a laugh. "No offense, Jill, but regression is chapter one in the textbook of male pseudo-analysis. Hell, it's more like the remedial course they give to stupid kids before they actually get into the real course."

Sarah quickly cut in. "Jill is so dead-on about this, Josh. I mean, you whine incessantly when you don't want to do something." She turned to Jill. "Last year, we were going to my friend Michelle's wedding. Josh complained all through the trip. His eggs were runny, his suit was itchy, the hotel wasn't good enough--"

Aaron tore through the dining room waving Amy's sippycup and his sister followed behind him, wailing. "Clara!" Jill yelled.

"Then today," Sarah continued, "he started calling me a K-I-K-E. He said that he and his little friend at work were trying to make everyone use it."

"Not everyone," said Josh. "Only Jews."

"Like the blacks," said Mark. "Oh, totally."

"Exactly. Wassup, my kike?" Josh said.

"You see?" Jill said, pointing a manicured finger at Josh. "Regression."

Josh turned to Mark. "Didn't I say I agreed?"

"It's the way you agreed," said Sarah. "So typical."

Jill patted Sarah's hand across the table. "This is all about having kids, you know."

Sarah dabbed her eyes with her napkin and bravely scooped another forkful of rice into her mouth. "This is absolutely fantastic," she said. "You have got teach me how to make it."

"Oh knock it off Sarah. The recipe is on the box," Josh said. "The only difference between Rice-a-Roni with fried beef in America and in Africa is that we don't have flies crawling on our faces here."

Aaron crawled out from beneath the table. He looked at Josh and smiled. "Kike," he said with a smile.

"I don't think he's ready for kids," Mark said.

Josh threw his hands up.

Sarah's face was flushed and she was having trouble catching her breath. Josh reached across the table to squeeze her hand but she jerked back. "I'm sorry," he said and looked down at his plate.

"Kike!" Aaron yelled.

"Clara!" Jill called, who emerged to escort Aaron back to the kitchen.

"Excuse me." Sarah stood up and went toward the bathroom. Jill followed her.

As silence descended, Mark gave Josh a coy smile and a shrug. "So anyway, kike," Mark laughed. "Raising a family has its perks."

Josh forced a smile, not sure if the word had lost its pleasure because he felt like a complete idiot or because he could not stand to hear it come from Mark.

"You know, kike, I think of you as a little brother."

"I'm older than you, Mark."

"Yeah, and if we had liver, we could make liver and onions, if we only had onions."

"What does that mean?"

"You see, that's what I'm talking about. You're lucky you didn't get the puppet treatment. But I have to say that Jill wasn't that far off. You regress."

"Why is this analyze-Josh night?"

"Hey, I'm not the one who walked in here calling everyone a kike."

"Funny, I don't remember it happening that way."

"What is it with you and kids? They're not as bad as they look and only half as bad as they smell. And besides all that good stuff you already know--about them being the most rewarding thing that will happen in your life -- it's not like you have to give up hookers or anything."

"I don't go to hookers, Mark."

"Yeah, right. Anyway, you're going to have to do it sooner or later. What's the big deal?"

"I will never go to hookers."

"I mean the kids. This year, next year, you're going to have a couple. And it really is pretty great, believe it or not. I mean, not as great as when you're in college and fucking two girls at once and you look up and see your friends have snuck into the closet to watch. But then, what could beat that?"

A long pause hung in the air. Mark held his satisfied grin and Josh suddenly became very aware of his breathing.

"Mark?"

"What?"

"Do you actually have any little brothers?"

"No."

"Good."

They heard the bathroom door open and Jill returned. She was staring straight ahead when she walked into the room, looking beyond Josh rather than at him. Josh tried to see if Sarah was following her, but Jill came in at a particular angle that blocked the hallway behind her.

"Josh, you need to go."

"Where's Sarah?"

"She's staying with us tonight."

Josh got up and started to walk toward the bathroom but Jill grabbed his arm.

"I think you should just go," she hissed.

Josh tried to soften his face, knowing that it was nearly impossible for him to elicit any sympathy from either Mark or Jill. But he tried anyway.

"Put yourself in my position for second, will you, Jill? I had a crappy day. Got punched in the face. Got psychoanalyzed over dinner and my wife is in the bathroom crying. Let me go talk to her."

"Go home, Josh."

"Sarah!" Josh called out. "I'm leaving. But only because Jill said you asked me to." He paused and turned his head so that his ear faced the hallway. There was an awful hush. He could hear the faint clamoring of cartoons coming from the playroom. He noticed that there were flowers on the dinner table. He had missed that before. Daisies.

They stood for almost a full minute in the hum of the television. Then Jill tugged at Josh's arm and motioned toward the door.

"Sorry, kike," Mark said.

"Yeah, me too."

The doorman opened the door for Josh and wished him a goodnight with a slight smirk, having seen his eye. How he hated being called sir. He walked into the street. The air was crisper than he remembered. He touched his eye and could feel a few millimeters of gushy swelling between the skin and the bone. Upstairs, Jill would be basking in Sarah's misery, playing the concerned confidant and reveling in the moment of being needed. Would Sarah remember Jill caused the fight in the first place?

Bestest friends.

He took a breath of cold air deep into his lungs and gazed up to where he figured the Lowensteins' balcony was. The moon hung behind the tall building. Josh was struck by the size of it. It cast a bright, nearly perfect reflection in the building's windows. Staring at the moon directly, he could clearly make out its shadowed, scarred surface.

He looked at the reflection for a long time. Why is it, he wondered, that you see some of life's most beautiful details only during quiet moments of suffering? It's as if things slow down and life syncs up with some somber soundtrack and you suddenly pay attention.

Before stepping off the curb, he felt a particular sensation washing over him. He knew what it was, though he dreaded to admit it.

It was relief.

This was probably the beginning of the end for him and Sarah. A sad thing, but for the best. He breathed in deeply. It was the finest breath he had taken in a long, long time.

He raised an arm and hailed a taxi.

THE COUP

In his fifty years as a synagogue member, Daniel Birnbaum had survived plenty of change. There had been births, deaths and at least two reupholsterings. He'd seen four rabbis come and go, and had withstood Ethel Weintraub's annual call to elect "young blood" onto the Board. Daniel was a man who could deal with change.

Daniel loved his congregation's service. It was a traditional ceremony where psalms, prayers, and the reading of the Torah pursued one another like a series of courses in a sumptuous feast; each part was savored in its own time, yet enhanced by the anticipation of something delicious still to come.

And each ritual had its own unique dependability. If asked what came to mind when the prayer *Anu Amecha* was sung on the High Holidays, Daniel was sure every member of the synagogue would say the same thing: Goldstein. For as long as Daniel could remember, Abe Goldstein's voice could be heard above everyone's during that prayer.

Likewise, Steve Bayer was the self-selected leader of *Aleinu*. Max Bloom sang harmony on *Adon Olam*. During the High Holidays, Fred Grossman and his son looked after *Avinu Malkheinu*. Judd Levy shushed everyone when the chatting became too loud. And Gerry Insler gave out candy to the kids. Everything and everyone had a place.

For nearly twenty years, the Birnbaum's responsibility was *Ein K'Eloheinu*, which Daniel took over when Mark Barton died. There was no issue that time. Barton was an old widower, whose children lived far away. Two Shabbats after his passing, Daniel simply stepped into the role without a word or fuss from anyone. He wasn't even sure anyone noticed. That is, except his two sons, who jumped to their feet and sung the prayer like two bold little crooners at his sides. By the time they were young men, still singing at his sides, Daniel was certain that the congregation was always pricked with a touch of Birnbaum envy whenever they thought of *Ein K'Eloheinu*.

And so it came with great surprise that after his son Avi went away to school, on a Saturday when his son Jacob was home with the flu, Ed Klein rose to challenge their station.

At first, when the congregation started to sing *Ein K'Eloheinu*, Daniel thought he was imagining the other loud voice. Avi and Jacob had always been next to him, so he was used to hearing them above the crowd. Standing there alone had caused him enough anxiety to wonder if he was hearing things. But by the third verse, it was clear that Ed and his son were chanting just a touch louder than everyone else, louder even than Daniel, and adding slightly more harmony than what was -- to him -- acceptable.

On the following Sabbath, with Jacob back at his side, Daniel was sure that the Kleins had increased their singing volume from slightly loud to just plain screaming.

He turned to Jacob but the confirmation he had expected to see in his son's eyes never materialized. Apparently, his friends were also oblivious to the assault.

When *Ein K'Eloheinu* was over, Jacob sat down and thumbed the prayer book, Mel Adler folded his tallis, and Mark Leifman and Fred Wasserman continued their conversation as they started to walk away.

How could they be missing this?

"An aynredenish iz erger vi a krenk," he said to himself, echoing his father's Yiddish. "A delusion is worse than a disease." He had to wake them up. Everything was going to be ruined.

When he confronted his friends about the Kleins' hostile takeover of *Ein K'Eloheinu* from the Birnbaums, he was met with bemused smiles and an accusation that he was overreacting. This put an end to his plan for a preemptive strike to squash the impending coup.

Daniel needed a secret weapon. He thought hard about it on the way home from synagogue. He kept coming back to one thing: Klein had one son, while Daniel had two. He needed Avi to come home for just one weekend. Together, the Birnbaums could put an end to the threat forever.

Every home has a unique smell that only visitors can detect. It was this smell that greeted Avi as he heaved his laundry bag into his parents' house. He inhaled the scent, noticing and dissecting it for the first time.

Silver polish and beef stew.

The silver polish was easy. Every Thursday his mother would rub away the tarnish from every utensil, candlestick and random artifact in the house.

The stew, however, was a mystery. His mother had never made stew before, yet the odor was overpowering. How could he have failed to notice it before? His mother's regimented menu had no place for stew and it was inconceivable that she had bumped off Friday night broiled chicken in the mere six weeks he'd been away. The stew smell must have been some aroma cocktail, forged by years of other dinner smells. Avi remembered the only time his mother had ventured beyond her standard dishes. She had made lasagna. The meal turned out fine but the switch had disrupted his father's biorhythms and in the two weeks that followed, the poor man had lost three sets of house keys, missed his stop on the train home, and sent about eighty dollars through the wash in his pants pockets.

Jacob bounded down the stairs and gave his brother a hug. He released him quickly. "So, the troops are home to put down the coup."

"Of course, what could I say?" Avi said.

"He's nuts, Avi."

"I know, but--"

"It's a prayer, Avi. You can't own it and you certainly can't steal it."

"I agree. But for a second, assume that Ed really is trying to take it over."

"Avi, if Ed is really trying to steal *Ein K'Eloheinu* from a man who doesn't own it, then Ed's even crazier than dad."

Avi knew all this, but what could he do? His father obviously spent their youth imagining that he and Jacob had a special passion for this prayer. Avi sang it, but so did everyone else. Still, this was not the time to fill his father in on the truth. Not that he was enthusiastic about getting caught in his delusional battle.

He tried to explain this to Jacob, who refused to discuss anything beyond their father's insanity and whether or not the solution involved medication.

That Sabbath, Avi was talking with a former classmate in the lobby of the synagogue when his father seized his arm.

"He's here," Daniel said coarsely, motioning toward Ed as he entered with his family.

Avi watched his father assess Klein's route through the crowd. Suddenly, he was being dragged to some point in Klein's trajectory.

"Ed, how are you?" Daniel said, tapping Ed as he passed. "You remember my son Avi, right? He's home from school."

Ed squinted at Avi, then nodded. "Sure. Hi, Avi, you know my son Nathan."

Avi took Nathan's hand, and the two boys passed empathetic smiles to one another.

"And this," Ed said, pulling a man forward, "is my dear friend Gene Sokol. He's thinking of joining our synagogue."

"How nice," Daniel said. "Welcome. What do you do, Gene?"

"I'm an opera singer," Gene said and bowed.

"Baritone," Ed added.

Daniel was motionless.

"Well, we're going to sit down," Ed said. "See you inside."

When Ed had vanished, Daniel turned to Avi. "A ringer. That sonofabitch brought a ringer."

Avi watched his father throughout the service. Daniel had been following along in his prayer book with one finger inserted on the page of *Ein K'Eloheinu*. When the congregation reached the *Mourners' Kaddish*, there was only one page left to go.

As the few bereaved voices recited the somber prayer, Avi felt a poke in his side. "Watch," his father whispered to him, and raised a finger, then suddenly tilted it to the pews to their right. As if acting on Daniel's cue, Jeremy Kogos supplied a sustained and supportive "*Amen*" from several rows behind.

The prayer was over.

Daniel flipped the page and signaled his troops for *Ein K'Eloheinu*.

Avi scanned the congregation to see who was watching. He opened his mouth to sing, but as he did, the booming baritone voice of the opera singer filled the sanctuary, silencing everyone else.

He looked at his father, whose face contorted as if he had just been shot in the back. The premature start was altogether unfair, but the deed was done.

Then Avi realized that not only had the Klein contingent's first note been early, but they were also singing *Ein K'Eloheinu* with a different *niggun*, a new melody. The coup was underway. The Birnbaum section, friends included, was silent. They were either unable to sing along with the brand new tune or simply too stunned that Daniel had been right from the start about the looming attack.

Suddenly, Avi heard a voice fall completely out of tune with the Kleins. A few people turned to see who was shouting a different song.

It was Jacob. He was leading the counterattack.

For a moment, Jacob was on his own. He was singing the old way and was almost completely drowned out by the Klein chorus. Then Mel Adler took a deep breath, put a hand on

Daniel's shoulder and joined in. The Grossmans followed. The Sterns. Then other friends nearby. By the time Avi started singing, the entire congregation had become a harmonious roar.

The coup was utterly squashed.

"Wow," the rabbi said, taking the podium. "Now that's what a prayer should sound like." Then he leaned forward and silenced the coup forever. "Thank you, Birnbaums, as always, for leading us in that one."

Avi felt his father squeeze his hand. He leaned back and winked at Jacob, who smiled. Even without that small token of recognition the boys had asked the rabbi to bestow, their father's place as the voice of *Ein K'Eloheinu* was secure.

HINENI

"Here I am, impoverished of deeds, trembling and frightened... I have come to stand and supplicate before You for Your people, who have sent me although I am unworthy and unqualified to do so."

-- The Chazzan's Song

On the 21st day of May in the year 1792 on the Gregorian calendar, corresponding to the 29th day of Ramadan in the year 1206 on the Hijri calendar, or the 29th day of Iyyar in the year 5552 on the Hebrew calendar, the world received the last of the great miracles.

There was an omen, of course, which was misinterpreted as a sign of something ominous to come. But prophecy can be imprecise.

It was the age of revolution. Leopold II had recently assumed the crown of the Holy Roman Emperor after the death of Joseph I. To the west, the French constitutional monarchy was crumbling and the life of Leopold's sister, Marie Antoinette, was in the hands of the Assembly. To the east, Catherine, the Empress of Russia, was an excuse away from invading the remnants of Poland, even as she unleashed her dogs on the

Ottomans.   In the center, Leopold tried to maintain the appearance of control as his monarchy teetered.

He presided over coronation festivities at the Nostitz Theatre in Prague, the highlight of which was Mozart's opera, *La Clemenza di Tito*, The Mercy of Titus.   It was commissioned for the occasion -- a transparent reminder that royalty can be benevolent.

For two audience members however, the subject gave their secret mission a hint of poetic retribution.

Late in the first act, four boxes from the stage, a corpulent woman rocked forward to the edge of her seat and gazed over the gilded railing of her nest.   She raised the stem of her opera glasses to her swollen face, scanning the heads of those below her and the faces in the balconies across the way.   She paused to gaze at a vacated box in the second tier and scoffed.   The box had just been occupied by two well dressed men.   She pursed her lips and tousled her gown like a hen ruffling her feathers.   She knew their type.   They hated the opera but loved to say they had been.   One needs to sit through the entire opera to pretend to adore it, she thought.   It's a test of endurance.

But she was wrong about these two.

They had come solely because the engagement offered a unique opportunity to steal something of great value -- a small stone, four inches long and two inches wide.   It was not precious or rare or exquisite in the ordinary sense of those terms. Nonetheless, to the two seekers, Baruch Avni and his son Shema, it was among the most exquisite objects in all of God's glorious collections.

For this stone had once been a part of a block in the high wall in the Greater House, the room just outside the Holy of Holies, the most sacred place in Solomon's Temple that had cradled the Ark of the Covenant.   And for the men in the Avni family, descendants of the masons who had built the Temple, these stones could sing.

Since the Temple's destruction, the Avni clan had been working to reunite all of the Temple's fragments, with generation after generation taking up the quest.

Those who labor with love impart to their work their very essence. And their work permeates their souls in return. The paint and canvas, clay and wheel, marble and chisel, seep deep into the artists' beings. And when the work one does is the work of God, the transfer is awesome indeed.

This truth has been celebrated by our greatest philosophers, from Socrates to Ibn Sina; simply put, there are many ways to divine reason, knowledge and love. And while the path is hard to find and difficult to follow, every once in a while someone finds his way, cracks open the door, and is granted an unfettered glimpse of Eternity.

It was so with the ancient Avnis. Trained by the Phoenicians to be master masons, their sweat drenched the raw slabs quarried from the Cave of Zedkiah. Their muscles cleaved the slabs into blocks, and their fingers gently caressed their cool surfaces. And as their work pervaded their souls, the family was blessed with a unique gift: they could hear the music of the stones of Solomon's Temple, hewn on the border between the mortal and the divine.

When Baruch spoke of their song he said that the stones sang not so much with a voice, or even a tune, but with a haunting melody that resonated like a heart filled with prayer.

Indeed, maybe it is better to say that the stones prayed.

How this particular fragment -- the one they sought -- had traveled from Jerusalem to Prague after the Temple's destruction and how it became part of a corbel in the basement of a theatre is a tale for another day.

What matters for our story is that the stone was here in Prague, and Baruch and Shema Avni were in pursuit of it.

Father and son walked down to the basement of the theatre. They had a floor plan to navigate the corridors but the stone's sonorous beacon guided them, growing louder with each step in the right direction.

When they reached a certain place beneath the stone, Baruch and Shema gazed up at a ledge below the corbel. Without a word, Baruch bent down and laced his fingers to create a foothold for the boy, heaving him up with a grunt of exertion.

Baruch remembered a time when he could carry Shema in a little, ingenious wooden box that had no bottom and was fitted with leather straps inside. Baruch could carry the box and Shema with no more trouble than carrying a small crate of potatoes. He would place the box over some spot on a walkway or hallway, and Shema, completely concealed, would chisel out a piece of the Temple from its resting place.

Shema grabbed onto the wall and pulled himself up, twisting his foot into Baruch's coat for traction and stepping onto his shoulders. Resting his hand against the bottom of the corbel, he closed his eyes and breathed in the stone's vibrations. He withdrew a small hammer and a metal spike from his coat pocket. Wrapping the spike in a rag, he leaned forward and placed its point into the mortar around the rock. He gave it a light tap and the mortar cracked like brittle chalk. He held the spike tightly in the rag and struck it gently, almost pushing the tool into the wall rather than pounding it. He blew into the crevice and brushed away the larger bits of dust. Nudging the spike again, he felt the rock move. It was like pushing on a child's loose tooth. He wiggled some more and it came free. Dust and crackle rained down on Baruch. Shema tapped his father with his toe to indicate that the stone was free, but Baruch already knew, having heard the stone's song open wide.

A light flickered in the hall and two shadows grew across the floor. Shema put the stone and tools in the rag and stuffed them into his coat, then dismounted from Baruch's shoulders.

The shadows blackened as a figure stepped forward from around the corner, followed closely by another. Because of the men's unusual height -- nearly seven feet -- their immense, spotless white garments reflected the dim lights of the hallway, giving father and son a clear view of their gaunt faces.

"Tall Brothers!" Baruch hissed to Shema, pulling him back down the hallway in the direction they had come. The giants took long strides in pursuit. Father and son raced through the halls and up a flight of stairs to the theatre lobby, where they slowed their pace so as not raise suspicion. They made their way to the exit, stepped out beneath the *porte cochere*, and ducked around the side of the building.

"How?" Baruch panted. He leaned forward and put his hands on his knees. "Come," he said, standing up straight. As he turned, he plunged squarely into the stomach of one of the Tall Brothers. Baruch thought he heard an echo pass through the man's body. He slowly looked up and saw the deep etchings that spread about the Tall Brother's sullen face, which was as dry and cracked as old clay.

Shema kicked the man hard in the knee, causing him to collapse. "Come!" Shema shouted, and the pair took off. They ran toward the river. Looking back over his shoulder, Shema could see one of the Tall Brothers coming after them. He ran -- or rather strode with the speed of someone running -- along the shadows of the buildings. The other man limped in the darkness behind them.

Shema started to speak when Baruch stopped short and swung his arm out to try to stop his son from taking another step. But the boy's momentum carried him into the street. He turned to see a speeding draycart approaching. The driver tried to swerve. The sharp turn cracked the axel, sending a load of casks tumbling over the cart's rails. One barrel hit Shema in the chest and knocked him flat. Another landed squarely on his stomach.

Baruch fell to his knees. Pushing the cask aside, he crumpled over his boy's broken chest. A small crowd gathered. Baruch cried out in anguish. Someone put a hand on his shoulder and tried to pull him off the boy. Baruch turned, looking into the shadows of the street where the two Tall Brothers silently stared at the scene. One of them slowly folded his hands across his chest and bowed his head. The other looked straight ahead.

Baruch dug inside Shema's coat and pulled out the stone. He stumbled to his feet. "This? This is what you want?" he screamed. He held the stone to throw it, but its song filled him as it neared his ear. His arm relaxed.

"Never!" he yelled.

Police whistles tooted. Baruch's false papers would never withstand the scrutiny of an investigator looking into the death of a boy. Even with the relatively liberal Czech Family Laws, a Jew involved with such a spectacle was not a good thing. He wrapped the stone, pushed it into his shirt, and ran off.

***

The city of Strasbourg rests on the French side of the Rhine River on the easternmost frontier of Prussia. Centuries earlier, Strasbourg was a political, economic, and cultural center. Then it lost its power to the plague. And when that happened, the sweet, peaceful streets of Strasbourg began to seethe with fear and hatred, which usually means trouble for the Jews. In 1348, more than two thousand Jews were burned alive on a fiery stage. From then until October 1791, a week after the National Assembly granted the Jews of France citizenship, the town was serenaded each night with the *Judenblos,* the "Jews' Call," a trumpet blast that reminded the good people of Strasbourg of Jewish treachery.

One month after the horns went quiet, in a small lodging outside the city walls, Hineni Avni finished his evening prayers. The room had grown dark and several candles were lit, placed in such a way as to ensure that their circles of light overlapped on the table where Hineni had been reading. He was home alone, as usual. His father was away again and the walk to his uncle's house could mean crossing paths with one of the roving gangs of Strasbourg bigots.

He slowly and devotedly closed the book in front of him, concentrating so hard he didn't hear the front door open.

"Hineni," his father said softly.

The boy spun around. It took a moment to recognize Baruch in the dim light of the room, but when it came to him that his father was home, he leapt forward, crashing into him with a fierce embrace.

Baruch apologized, having had no way to avoid startling Hineni once he had entered. Baruch placed his hand on the boy's head and nestled him into his chest, feeling his body quake.

"Uncle gave you my letter, then?"

Hineni nodded.

"I'm sorry to tell you by letter but I thought it best. I was... well... I just thought it better than you expecting to see Shema come in behind me." Baruch remembered returning home four years earlier, learning as he entered of his wife's sudden death while he was away.

Hineni released himself from his father, and wiped the tears from his cheeks. "Uncle gave me letters for you," he said. "I'll get them."

He returned a moment later with three sealed envelopes.

Baruch looked at the wax seals. One letter was from Persia, surely confirming that the Prague stone had been received. The Avnis sent recovered stones to Babylon, the place where their ancestors had first carried the remnants of the temple after being expelled by Nebuchadnezzar from Jerusalem.

The second letter was from Jerusalem. It was from the Seer, the Avni cousin who received visions of the locations of stones. Baruch started to break the seal when he noticed the third letter was from Prague.

He tore it open and unfolded the piece of calfskin vellum inside. Three rose petals fell into his lap. Baruch sighed loudly.

"What is it?" asked Hineni.

"It is from the Tall Brothers," he said. "They wrote to let me know that in keeping with both the Jewish and ancient Christian customs, they guarded Shema's body from the time of death."

"But your letter said they killed him. Why would they--"

Baruch cut him off. "The Tall Brothers didn't mean to kill Shema. It was an accident."

"You wrote that they chased you. You may call it an accident, but--"

Baruch waved him off, reminding him with a motion that the Tall Brothers would never kill someone purposely. They were Ascetics -- followers of an ancient teacher named Origen who believed that the Spirit of God, the Church of Christ, was scattered throughout the world after his death and lives on in each of us. Origen believed that the destruction of Solomon's Temple was connected in this way to Christ, as when Christ said of his impending death, "destroy this Temple and in three days I will raise it up."

The parallel was obvious to the Tall Brothers: in seeking to rejoin the scattered pieces of the Temple, the Avni clan was rejoining Christ himself -- resurrecting him, so to speak. And anyone other than God who attempted such a feat would be committing an awesome profanity -- one that might even prevent the true resurrection of Christ.

"For their stupid metaphor," Hineni scoffed, "Shema is dead?"

"Religion is like that. Many wars have been waged over much less."

"What if they are right? What if we are resurrecting Jesus?"

"I don't believe what they believe."

Hineni considered this for a moment. "Do they know about the song of the stones?"

"Only through us. They can't hear it."

"Then why should they believe we can hear it?"

"When they first learned of our quest, they were probably just curious. Then they must have intercepted one of the stones we found. Jerusalem stone is quite obvious to those who know of it. They had no other explanation as to how we were able to locate them -- they had to concede that our gift is real."

"But that's proof of a gift from God. Isn't it His will that we seek the Temple? They should help us."

Baruch looked at his son and smiled. "You are too smart. I don't have all the answers. They must think we are misusing this gift and that it will lead us all to ruin."

Baruch beckoned Hineni to the table. The boy dropped into a chair as his father withdrew a small bundle wrapped in a scrap of homespun wool from a drawer. He placed it gently onto the table. Hineni lowered his eyes. One by one, Baruch placed three small stones in front of his son.

Hineni knew this game all too well. It filled his earliest memories. His father would ask, "Which stone sings?" Hineni could only guess and he usually guessed wrong.

Hineni closed his eyes, held his hand out over the table and concentrated. He sensed the faintest breeze on his fingertips. He lowered his hand and laughed at himself, opening his eyes to see his hand splayed across a bare space on the table; the closest stone was about four inches to the side.

"Belief," Baruch said, which was a short way of reminding Hineni that he needed to believe more strongly in the songs to hear them.

"But I do believe," Hineni insisted.

"No. You profess belief. Too many people profess belief but do not truly believe. There was a time when we really believed and wondrous things occurred. Moses led us from Egypt; Jesus spurned the Romans; Mohammed rode through Mecca. These prophets were willed into existence by belief and need. Now, we mostly profess. We must return to belief or we Jews will forever seek freedom, Christians will forever quest for peace, and Mohammedans will forever battle for respect. You need to believe, Hineni. Or you will never hear the songs."

Baruch opened the letter from Jerusalem. The Seer had written it in code, listing the locations of two stones Baruch was to find and providing instructions on how to access the underground banking network.

"I'm going to a town called Riva del Garda in the Venetian Republic," he told his son, "and then to Theosebos, a city on the coast north of Dubruvnik."

"May I come?" Hineni asked.

Baruch looked at his son and shook his head. "You are too young."

Hineni gazed down at the table. This was not a question of age. His father thought he would be of no value, or worse, a burden. Suddenly, Hineni slammed his fists against his ears. He hit them again as Baruch grabbed him from behind and forced his arms down.

"This is not the way," Baruch said, holding the boy close.

"Maybe this is exactly the way." Hineni's face crinkled like a drying apple and he started shaking. "I don't want to be the One," he said. His father held him tighter.

The One was the deaf Avni son. Three hundred years ago, a prophesy had been told in a London street. According to family legend, an Avni long ago had stepped around a heap of rubbish spilling across his path and felt something snag his ankle. He looked down to find an old woman nestled with her back against the dross and clothed in what appeared to be a woven rug.

She raised her head toward him, revealing a polluted face and clouded eyes so gruesome that he winced.

"Yehudah," the woman rasped.

The Avni ancestor shook with fear at being pegged as a Jew by the blind woman.

"Yehudah," she repeated louder. "Gawd's song wilt end wit the boy wit no ears." She opened her mouth and became as still as a clay doll. From her unmoving mouth echoed the song of the stone. The Avni ancestor moved closer, but the fragile old woman vanished.

For several generations hence, each Avni took hold of his new born son and checked to see if the boy had ears. One year, an Avni was born who could not hear the song of the stones. The family realized that the prophesy of having "no ears" could be metaphorical and the extended family grieved and prayed. One day, with no prior warning, the boy's ears opened. And not only could he hear the song, but he also had the gift to see paths leading to stones, which he described as a golden spider web spun out before him. He was the first Seer.

Since then, twelve Avni boys had been born deaf to the stones. In each case, when the child finally acquired the gift, it was accompanied by some other amazing power. But the prophesy said that the song would one day end, which meant that Hineni had more to fear than to look forward to.

"I want to come with you," Hineni pleaded. "Maybe I cannot hear the song, but I can carry things and you said once to mother that having Shema with you made people less suspicious. You said, 'no Jew would parade their child around to be arrested or beaten by a gang.'"

"It's too dangerous. See what taking Shema got me?"

"Please, father. We need this. You said that you had two stops. Let me come to the first and then I will come home if I am a burden."

"Let us sleep on it," Baruch said.

Two weeks later, Baruch and Hineni set off, accepting a ride on their neighbor's cart atop a pile of prickly hop bines. The neighbor took them as far as Colmar, south of Strasbourg. From there, the father and son headed further south and east, following the Rhine into Switzerland.

Place names swirled in Hineni's head. He had been studying their route -- every region, every river, and every town -- since the morning Baruch had sat him down and laid out their plan. There was no further discussion about whether or not Hineni should join his father; Baruch had simply laid out a map of Europe and begun to prepare his younger son.

Hineni had studied the map carefully. Judging the span between the cities, he figured that Riva del Garda could take more than a month to get to, even if the weather cooperated. Reaching Theosebos could take another month or so.

He had also been practicing to play the part of a Roman Catholic since Baruch said that the waves of French Catholics fleeing Napoleon to parts of Northern Italy provided excellent cover. Baruch, alias, Nicholas Sinclair, was to be a recusant priest who had denounced the new French constitution, expressed support for the Pope, and refused to write the oath of allegiance to the new government. He was accompanied by his attendant Antoine.

Baruch explained to Hineni that he had selected the monikers for Saint Nicholas of Myra, the patron saint of thieves, and Saint Antoine of Padua, patron saint of lost items -- perfect spirits for their mission. Baruch taught him a number of Catholic prayers and stories about the saints.

The next several weeks brought Hineni a new life. It was as if he had cracked open an ordinary egg and glistening gems had spilled forth. The world was full of such beauty that it brought him to tears. He stood over a lake one night and said his prayers as the sun set behind the mountains. When he opened his eyes, the sky had turned the color of a blacksmith's blast furnace, dripping molten heaven into the folds of the earth.

He whispered in Hebrew, "How great are your works, God, You make them all with wisdom; the world is full of your possessions."

Several days later, while walking on a mountain path that lay before him like a strip of ribbon, Hineni stopped and gazed down into the valley. The trees below echoed with bird songs and the water in the lake was so clear, Hineni could see both the reflection of the trees and the bottom of the lake at once.

"The whole world is full of God," Hineni said to himself.

Baruch watched his son staring down at the forest. After a moment, he spoke softly. "They say that somewhere upon this earth is the Forest of God, where he grows the trees that bind Him to His people. Every religion has its own tree. The oldest ones are so tall that the tops cannot be seen. Others are just saplings, having grown from seeds that fell from older trees. The trees live side-by-side, either growing together in harmony or strangling each other's roots.

"At the center of this forest is a very special tree. God tends to it with the utmost care, showering it with nourishing water and causing the worms to soften the earth below. Of course, the other trees are jealous of this one. They try to burrow their roots beneath it to steal its water, and send branches over it to gather its sunlight. But the more they pain this tree, the harder it becomes to destroy. Instead of starving, the tree draws upon itself, strengthening its limbs until they are like iron."

"It is us," Hineni said.

"Yes. It is the tree of the Jews."

Hineni stared silently for a moment. A breeze passed over the treetops below. "It is no wonder everyone hates us," he said finally.

"It is hard not to be envious--"

"It is not God's love that they envy," Hineni said, cutting his father off. "It is our arrogance. Who else would tell such a story?"

Baruch laughed loudly and put a hand on his son's shoulder. "Hineni, I have heard that story told by Christians, Mohammedans, Zoroastrians, Shamans, Sunnis, Sufis and Druze. The only difference in each of their stories is the name of the tree in the center."

They arrived on the outskirts of Riva del Garda in late December. After several weeks of biting cold, the damp air of the southern Italian Alps felt like slipping into a warm bath. Hineni filled his lungs with cool mountain air. The mist turned to droplets in his nose, making it run. He remembered a spring evening when he was about six years old. His father was away, as usual, and his mother had brought home a bundle of blossoming Gewürztraminer buds that she said a man at the market had given her in return for having glimpsed her beautiful face. She glowed as she arranged the grape vines.

Baruch and Hineni arrived at a stone farmhouse. "This is it," Baruch said.

Hineni gazed down upon the landscape, which looked like a billowing blanket of green. He recalled a line from one of Solomon's songs, something about God leaping upon the mountains and skipping upon the hills. He pictured God rejoicing among his creations.

A man and woman approached them. Baruch told them the story of Nicolas Sinclair, purposefully fumbling for Italian words he knew well to make it seem more plausible he was here by necessity and chance. He told them about their flight from France. He explained that he was a skilled stonemason and that in return for boarding, for which he could not pay, he would trace their entire stone fence in the morning and fix any deficiencies.

The couple, Leone and Mara, were farmhands in charge of the cows. Leone offered to make an introduction to the farm owner. He was sure that the owner would provide them a place for the night, "Since," he whispered, "the fence is in need of much work."

Leone and Mara left to fetch the farm owner while Baruch told Hineni what had transpired. They practiced their story again.

Leone and Mara returned with good news: Nicholas and Antoine could stay in the room above the barn and were welcome to eat with the farmhands at dinner. Baruch thanked them profusely, translating for Hineni as Leone led them up steep wooden stairs to a room above the barn.

Hineni looked around the room. Aside from three wooden planks along the walls that were used for sleeping, the room was bare. He noticed a thick, musty smell of wet wood mixed with a faint whiff of liquor.

Two hours later, Leone roused Baruch and Hineni from deep slumbers to come down for some dinner. The three of them went to Leone and Mara's small quarters for a light Tyrolean meal of bread, cheese, roasted chestnuts and baked apple. "Antoine," Leone said to Hineni as he took another bite of the baked apple. "A good name and a good saint." Baruch translated for Hineni, who smiled at Leone and went back to his food.

Leone continued speaking with Baruch. "Antoine, the Saint of Padua, saint of lost things, shipwrecks and oppressed people." He finished his statement with a satisfying crunch on a piece of bread.

"He knows all the patron saints," Mara offered.

Leone puffed up slightly. "Not all," he said with a sly smile. "But many. Go ahead, ask me one."

Baruch asked him the patronage of Paul.

"Oh, please. A harder one than the patron of Umbria and snakes."

Matthew?

"Salerno and book keepers," Leone said, raising an eye.

Fever?

Abraham.

Francis Assisi?

Families.

Misfortune?

Agricola of Avignon.

Hineni looked back and forth between the two men as Baruch lobbed names, places and afflictions. The quiz seemed to have turned into a dance, with Leone following Baruch's lead, answering his questions almost before he finished the words.

Edwin?

Homelessness.

Palestine?

George.

Baruch let out a grunt of approval. Mara took hold of Leone's hand and the four people sat in silence for a moment until Mara asked Hineni if he wanted another baked apple. Hineni's eyes blinked rapidly. Something had changed among the adults, but he wasn't sure what it was. Their shoulders appeared to have loosened and they all sank a little deeper into their seats. Hineni tried to catch Baruch's eye but his father had turned back to his cheese.

The walk back to the barn could not come quickly enough for Hineni. It had started to rain while they were inside, and the soft, wet mountain turf gave under their feet. As soon as they were near the barn, Hineni asked Baruch what he had missed in the conversation.

Baruch bent down, straightened the cuff of his pants, and retied his bootlace. He murmured something.

"What?" Hineni said.

Baruch looked over his shoulder. "Help me fix my boot," he said.

Hineni groaned and bent down to hold Baruch's lace in place as he tied a bow around his finger. Baruch leaned forward and whispered, "They are Jews."

"What?"

"Shhh," the father said. "They are Jews. Probably Marranos from Spain or forced converts from the Paduan Ghetto."

"How do you know?"

"The saints. It's our code."

Baruch was asleep almost as soon as he pulled his pony-skin blanket over his body.

Hineni fell asleep thinking about the codes, which gave way to visions of people hiding in the shadows of alleys made of Temple stones. There were no markers but he sensed, somehow, that the people were Jews, Muslims, Christians, Buddhists, and Hindus, and thousands of other religions he could not name. All were deaf and scared and oblivious to the sound of the walls that only Hineni seemed to hear. But the sound was not musical; it was a cracking, like the sound a frozen lake makes when it is stood upon. The cracking soon grew to a rumble and then, with a thunderous roar and a whoosh like the sound of a million birds taking flight, the walls fell upon all of the people but him.

Hineni woke up panting. He took several hard unsatisfying breaths.

The sun barely glowed above the horizon when Leone noisily climbed the steps in the barn to rouse the guests. After a swift breakfast, Leone, Baruch and Hineni set out to survey the estate's stone fence on horseback. The morning mist was heavy and condensed on the backs of the horses like a thin patina of moss. Mud oozed around the horses' hooves with each step.

The dry-stone fence they followed was only about two feet high. Leone explained that these types of enclosures were not common in the area, since animals were typically grazed freely. But some people, like his master, simply like fences.

Baruch stopped and dismounted. He called Hineni and Leone to the wall. "Look here," he said, pointing out a place where the wall transformed from a single pile of flat rocks to a double wall structure built with rounder rocks.

Baruch said that whoever commissioned the fence had brought in skilled builders who knew how to work with what was here.

Baruch continued along the wall, making comments about the integrity of the structure and what needed to be done. Along one particular section that stood about three feet tall, Leone pointed out a heap of stones that rested on either side of the fence. Baruch leaned in, plucked a few stones from the piles, and placed them together as if trying to refit pieces of a broken vase. "These extra stones," he said, "are from a stile, not the fence. No need to worry about this part."

Hineni watched his father's inspection carefully. Sometimes Baruch would walk backwards twenty or thirty paces from the fence to see how level it was. At other times he got on his hands and knees and rested his nose against the rocks as if he could smell a deficiency. He talked about the fence and its stones. He pointed out which stones had come from a coastal area, and which had come from the mountains. He expounded on various types of walls, describing mortars made from mud or gypsum or volcanic ash.

Hineni did not understand everything, because Baruch did not translate everything back to French for him. But he knew the chatter was part of the ruse. In their time together, Hineni had learned a lot about what it takes to gain people's trust from his father. He had seen Baruch concoct extraordinary stories when they needed to stay overnight at an inn, or enter a city after dark, or rid themselves of a would-be thief by dispatching him to rob a phantom coach due in at such–and-such hour. The purpose of his stories about rocks and walls was to ensure that by the time they located the one stone they were seeking, Leone would be so bored that whatever Baruch said or did would mean nothing to him.

Baruch coughed loudly. It was the signal.

They were near.

Baruch dismounted. He stood next to his horse for a moment, walking slowly toward the fence as if measuring his steps. His entire body, not just his eyes, seemed fixed on a single point.

"What is it?" Leone asked.

Baruch did not answer. He placed his hands gently on the top of the fence and closed his eyes.

"Looks sturdy to me," Leone said.

"This section is going to fall," Baruch answered, slightly louder than before. "Come, put your hands on it."

Leone dismounted and stood opposite Baruch. He placed his hands on the fence where Baruch had rested his fingers. "You're the expert," he said. "But it feels solid to me."

"No, I will show you." Baruch started to disassemble the fence, stone by stone. He carefully laid them on the ground in a neat row, following the order in which he was taking them down. He started a second row of rocks and then a third. Leone and Hineni watched closely. Baruch stopped on the fourth row of stones. He rearranged a few rocks still resting in the fence, tapped them, and flipped one upside down. "That was the problem," he said. "Now I must put it back together. It will be quite a while."

Hineni grew tired of the sound of rocks being placed upon one another.

Baruch seemed unsatisfied with the slightest wobble or quiver. Slowly, monotonously, he worked, placing and replacing stones. "There is a story in the Quran, the book of the Mohammedans," Baruch said. "Moses was traveling with an angel. He watched the angel sink a fishing boat owned by poor villagers, kill an innocent boy, and then rebuild a wall for some people who refused him food and shelter. Moses questioned the angel about these deeds. The angel said he sank the boat to save the villagers from a king who would have killed them for it; he killed the boy to save the next generation from his evil; and he rebuilt the wall to hide a treasure that was not meant for such hardhearted people." Baruch paused and looked lovingly at his work. He leaned forward against the fence, pushing it with all his weight. He looked up at Leone on his horse and smiled. "I hope that I have not hidden any treasure from you, Leone."

"It would not belong to me," Leone laughed. He dismounted and came over to give Baruch a drink of wine from his pouch. He handed him the skin and climbed onto the fence. "Very sturdy," he said, looking down at Baruch. "Nicholas, you appear to have left a few stones out. Should we find a place for them?"

Baruch looked around about his feet. There were indeed several stones sitting in the grass near the wall. "Well--" he said, but he was cut off by a loud whinny and a cry from Hineni. The two men looked up to see Hineni thrown from his horse. Leone leapt off the fence with Baruch right behind him. Hineni was on his back, but unharmed. Leone administered some wine and Hineni slowly got to his feet.

Leone went to fetch Hineni's horse. "Did you get it?" Hineni muttered. Baruch thought for a moment. The fall -- it had been a trick to distract Leone from the stones on the ground. He smiled at his son and rubbed his head. "I'll come back for it."

They mounted their horses and headed back towards the farmhouse. Soon after they crested a small hill, Baruch said he had left something where he had been working. He turned around to get it. Leone turned as well, even though Baruch insisted that he would meet them back at the barn. As they again reached the top of the hill, they could see all the way down to where Baruch had just repaired the fence. There was a man there.

Baruch cracked his horse's hind quarters with an open palm and immediately opened to a gallop. Leone and Hineni followed but they could not keep up. Baruch streamed across the field at full speed. Hineni looked at the man near the fence. His heart sank and he dug his heels into the sides of his horse. The man was wearing a white robe.

The man heard the gallop of approaching horses and fled into the woods, disappearing into the trees. By the time Baruch forced his horse into a spectacular jump over the fence, the Tall Brother had vanished.

Hineni and Leone reached the fence. Hineni looked at the ground where his father had been working. Nothing. The Tall Brother had taken all the leftover rocks.

Hineni prodded his horse around and then headed straight for the fence. He had never made a horse jump before. He galloped with his eyes wide open, kicking at the horse. The fence came up quickly as Hineni yelled in the strongest, deepest voice he could muster and the horse leapt as if its legs were Hineni's to rule. They came down on the other side without missing a stride and Hineni rode straight into the woods.

He saw no one. He called out, but no sound was returned. He rode through the woods for quite a long time before giving up and turning his horse around.

As soon as he emerged from the trees, he heard his father's voice. He was yelling. Hineni saw his father, still on horseback, facing Leone and screaming at him. Italian and French are close enough that Hineni understood the one word Baruch repeated over and over again. *Perchè?* Why?

Leone sat hunched in his saddle, staring at the ground.

"You don't know what you've done," Baruch said.

"I do," Leone murmured. "They came two nights before you." He looked over his shoulder and then turned back. "They said they know that Mara and I are Jews."

Baruch just shook his head. Whatever the consequences Leone and Mara would have suffered had their master learned they were Jews meant nothing compared to the sacrifices the Avni family had given through the centuries.

They rode back to the farmhouse in silence and Baruch and Hineni took their leave.

Baruch did not speak for several days. They walked each day for long stretches without eating or stopping. When they did pause, it was unexpectedly. Baruch would just stop walking. He'd sit and stare off for the duration of their rest. Hineni would quickly dart into the woods to relieve himself or rummage through their belongings to pull out some stale bread. Each time he offered food to his father, Baruch would sigh or pick up and start walking again, as if the food made him conscious of wasted time.

They took a rest outside a small town on their way to Theosebos. Hineni sat on a rock, considering what losing that one stone to the Tall Brother would mean for the plan to reunify the Temple. It was impossible for the entire Temple to be found and congregated, he thought. Over so many years, there had to be stones that were ground down to sand and swallowed by chickens, or dropped in the sea, or shoveled into the blast furnace of a glass blower.

He wished to tell his father this thought -- as if it would comfort him to know that he wouldn't find all the stones anyway. And then he thought better of it. He figured that his father would simply counter with a quote from some ancient text to explain it away -- one more parable to shed light on the never ending search for Truth.

Hineni saw his father pick a poppy from the ground and stare at it for a while. "One plus two is three. Two plus three is five. Three plus five is eight. Five plus eight is thirteen. And so on. The number of petals in a flower are most often in that sequence. Buttercups, five. Daisies, thirty-four or fifty-five."

"What does it mean?" Hineni asked, dispassionately. He was thinking, my father has barely spoken in days, and these are his first words?

"There are some people," said Baruch, "who believe that numbers come from a mystical place between man and the secrets of the universe; that they are not invented so much as they are discovered, plucked like butterflies from the air to those who can see them." He paused. "These flowers," he said, holding the poppy up to the sun to look at its glow, "are touched by something extraordinary."

He reached into his pocket and withdrew something wrapped in a piece of white cloth. "We must find a friend to take care of this." He laid the package on his lap and unwrapped it with great care.

Hineni's eyes opened wide when the stone was uncovered.

"You hear nothing?" Baruch asked Hineni.

"I thought the Tall Brother..."

Baruch sighed. All this time, he'd had it in his pocket and the boy heard nothing. "I followed him into the woods. He was way ahead and well hidden. But the fool might as well have been a belled mouse with this stone in his pocket."

"How did you get it from him?" Hineni asked. His father raised the rock to his ear and closed his eyes.

They arrived in the port town of Theosebos in the late afternoon, greeted by the delicious smell of a spring afternoon. Because it was a seaport, the air was purified by the salty breeze and the spices sitting on the docks. The city bustled with people as goods passed to and from the ships. The constant drone of cartwheels clanking over cobblestones was peppered with the shouts of merchants and dock workers, and an occasional mule bray. Some bells rang.

The rush of the streets made Hineni think of scurrying and swarming creatures found on a fallen tree. As a port, Theosebos was more a part of the Mediterranean trade industry than it was part of any particular country. A surveyor would be hard pressed to find three men in ten who saluted the same flag. Hineni saw people he had heard about, but thought were as imaginary as unicorns or fairies; people with skin the color of coffee beans and women with tattoos dotting their faces. He saw men clothed in sackcloth exchanging what looked like enough money to buy an entire town, and others in regal vestments hauling oak barrels.

His father stopped and bought two rings of bread studded with sesame seeds. Hineni bit into his bread and remembered a day he'd spent picnicking with his mother. She had brought strawberries. Hineni remembered sitting with his mother in the sun and the warm air, thinking that those were the finest strawberries he'd ever eaten. And now it occurred to him that no other piece of bread would ever taste as good as this sesame ring.

Baruch talked to the bread salesman for a bit. Then he relayed to Hineni that several ships from the French Navy had appeared that morning in the harbor, apparently come to investigate the sinking of a merchant ship off the coast. There was much concern. The French had recently declared war on Austria and the entire region feared the brutality of the French forces.

Baruch stopped a man and asked him something. The man pointed nonchalantly down a street. Baruch pulled Hineni behind him and turned down a narrow alley.

Hineni looked around. To the left he noticed a similarly narrow alley framed by a wrought-iron gate. Peering through the gate down the darkly lit street, he could make out something written on the wall in characters he had not seen in months. It was Hebrew and he could make out a *Kaf* and a *Shin*.

The *Ghetto*.

A fruitmonger rolled his barrow loaded with produce passed the gates. Hineni turned and followed his father into the hotel, stumbling over a tattered rug as he crossed the threshold. He looked back at the rug and suddenly noticed a woman sitting out on the street, next to the iron gates. Her back was pressed against a wall that dripped with green mold and pigeon feces. She turned slightly to face Hineni and he saw that her eyes were completely clouded.

"*Yahūdiyy*," she said. The word was close enough to the Hebrew word for Jew that Hineni understood. She opened her mouth, but emitted no sound. Then the edges of her mouth turned up into a slight smile.

A thought crossed Hineni's mind. He turned around quickly to see if his father had seen the woman, but Baruch was talking to the men inside. When Hineni looked back out the door, she was gone.

"Antoine!" Baruch barked from inside the inn.

The main entrance was small. Two old men sat facing each other in sagging wicker chairs with a game board squeezed between their legs. One of the men said something to Hineni.

"He thinks we are from the French ships," Baruch said.

"What should I say?"

"Nothing. Just show him your shoes. He thinks he can tell by our shoes if we're from the ships. Makes no sense, but do it anyway. Just don't show him your soles -- some people take offense to that."

Hineni lifted his foot and rotated it.

The man held out a tea stained hand and Baruch placed a coin in it. The man mumbled something. Baruch bowed awkwardly and motioned to Hineni to exit.

They climbed a flight of stairs and found three small private rooms at the top of the landing. Baruch looked in each room and picked one. He walked to the window and Hineni joined him and looked out. Three men walked through the gates of the Ghetto just below.

Hineni sat down on the bed.

Baruch continued to look out the window. "Can you hear it?" he asked.

"Is it close?" Hineni asked quietly.

Baruch sighed. "It is in the synagogue in the Ghetto. When it is quiet, you can hear it singing from across the way, echoing through the streets. It is so beautiful, Hineni."

They sat down together and Baruch set out the plan. It was illegal for non-Jews to enter the Ghetto at night. However, they were permitted to go in to seek a doctor. Hineni would fake stomach pains that evening. Baruch showed him exactly where the pain should be and how he should react when touched in different places.

"But how can we steal from a synagogue?" Hineni asked. Baruch assured him it was not stealing, it was taking back. "Then why can't we just ask for it?"

Baruch laughed. "What shall we say, 'would you mind if we were to chisel a piece of Solomon's Temple from your floor'?"

Hineni was unconvinced, but what could he do? Shema wouldn't have raised such questions. And after all, they were just rocks.

Baruch left to determine their best route for escape. Night fell and Hineni tried to fight his advancing sleep but his travels had made him too weary. He closed his eyes. In the onset of sleep, the creak of the door sounded to him like the moan of a cat. His father entered and Hineni woke with a soft yelp.

"They are here," Baruch said. "Tall Brothers."

"How do you know?"

"They left these by the door." He let a handful of rose petals fall to the floor.

"Why did they tell us? Is it a warning?"

"I think it is a plea. They wish to stop but cannot as long as we continue."

Baruch said that he had purchased a small rowboat. It was moored about three hundred yards from the Ghetto gate. They would slip out of the city after they had acquired the stone, and in the worst case, they could drop their disguises and row out to the French navy ships in the harbor and secure passage back home.

Later that night, Baruch decided it was time. They quietly slipped from the hotel and walked down to the dock. They placed their things in the rowboat. The streets were quiet with the exception of several drunks who meandered about, singing and urinating.

They made their way back, pausing briefly at the Ghetto gates. Baruch looked at Hineni. "Ready?"

Hineni nodded, hunched over and started to moan.

Baruch shouldered his arm to hold him up. He was a good actor, Baruch thought. The boy interrupted his moans to plead with his father for comfort. His addition of a limp was inspired.

They approached the Ghetto gates, which were closed but not locked. Baruch pushed through and called out for help in French, then Greek, then Arabic. He walked Hineni to the synagogue door and banged on it.

A man called out in Greek, "What is it?"

"My son, he is sick," Baruch responded.

Hineni whimpered and groaned.

A face appeared above them in a window. Footsteps echoed in an empty corridor. The locks of the door jingled and the man pulled the synagogue door open from the inside. "Doctor there," he said, believing Baruch to have trouble with Greek. He pointed down the street.

Baruch motioned that the boy needed to lie down. "Sick much."

The man looked at Hineni, who was bent over, barely hanging onto his father's shoulders. Baruch could see the fear in the man's face and the turmoil raging in his heart. It could be a trick, but the boy might very well be sick. Turning them away could bring the wrath of the police down upon him in the morning. He could let them in, but what if they were planning to burn the place to the ground? In the end, the man must have decided, happier the fool than a fiend. He opened the door fully and lifted Hineni's other arm around his shoulder. They carried him up a flight of wooden stairs and into the main sanctuary.

Hineni eyed the mezuzah on the doorpost. It was the first one he had seen in months and he longed to reach out and kiss it. They laid him down on a well worn pew. Hineni could smell the musty wood beneath him. The man lit a lamp and Hineni saw the dark blue hue of the ceiling, painted with stars. It was beautiful.

The man said he would return in a moment with the doctor. He looked back several times as he exited the room.

"Please be quick," Baruch said, and the man turned and left with haste. They listened as he descended the wooden steps.

"Do not stop moaning, Hineni," Baruch said as he withdrew several tools from the inside of his jacket.

Hineni continued his performance and rolled onto his side to see more of the synagogue. It was dark but he could make out the delicately carved wooden *bimah*, behind which were two fat, twisting columns. Between the two columns was the Ark, with wisps of plaster around the wood and a red velvet curtain hanging down in front of the Torahs.

Baruch moved to the side of the synagogue opposite where Hineni was lying. He crouched down in front of a pew in the center of the room and reached behind it to touch the wall. Wrapping his spike with a woolen cloth, he tapped the wall several times with a small hammer. He laughed softly. "Done," he said.

Hineni sat up. "You have it?"

"Yes. It was loose already. Let's go."

"But the--"

"Come Hineni, get up."

At that moment, there was a large, echoing sound and the building shook. Dogs began to bark. A bell started to chime frantically. There was another blast.

Baruch grabbed Hineni by the arm and pulled him down the synagogue steps. The man and the doctor stood at the entrance of the synagogue.

"What is it?" Baruch said.

"It is the French ships," the man said. "They are firing their cannons at us."

Baruch looked up at the night sky, above the low buildings in the Ghetto. There was a whistle and another blast. Before the echo ceased, another whistle cut through the air and a bomb detonated just outside the Ghetto, illuminating the dirty street as if it were mid-afternoon. Women screamed, babies cried and the dogs continued to wail. Another hit.

The man came to Baruch's side. "The boy, how is he?"

Baruch put a hand on the man's shoulder. "He will be fine. A bad stomach ache. Go, help the others."

People began to enter the Ghetto. Some ran in carrying children, others dragged themselves through the gates. They cried out in many languages but their pleadings were all the same: "Doctor!"

Soon, the tiny Ghetto street was filled with bloodied bodies and the people who carried them in.

The Ghetto had fourteen structures that housed thirty families. There were only two doctors in the community, yet everyone was out in the street, tending to anyone who needed help. They ran in and out of their homes, fetching blankets, water, candles, rags. More blasts. Some close, some far. More people piled into the Ghetto.

Baruch grabbed Hineni's arm and pulled him toward the Ghetto gates. "We must go!" he yelled over another explosion.

Hineni's feet were like weights. He could not move. It was not fear, it was guilt -- he was paralyzed by it. He had lied to get into the Ghetto and now, when he was in the midst of its pain, he was about to run off. His father helped him with his decision by yanking him forward.

As they exited the Ghetto, Baruch peered up and down the streets. Despite the chaos, he was able to maintain a level of urgent, but calculating control. He knew rowing out to sea now would be suicide. The French guns would be trained on any craft that left the shore. They just needed to get away from the targets and wait out the attack. In the morning, they would go to the dock and collect their belongings.

Then they saw the Tall Brothers. There were four of them, two up the street and two down, blocking their way and kneeling. Hineni looked more carefully. Their eyes were closed. They sat with their hands resting gently on their knees and their long legs tucked under them. In the middle of the mayhem they were at peace, like four birds in a storm, floating with the wind rather than against it.

A shell hit the roof of a nearby building and the force of the explosion knocked most of the people in the street to the ground. The noise came over Hineni like a wave of hot air. For a moment, everything slowed. People opened their mouths to speak or scream as fragments of the building rained down. For Hineni, there was nothing but silence. It was as if his head were encased in sand or stone.

A woman dressed in a brown aba patched with bits of checkered cloth ran toward him with a baby in her arms. She was screaming, yelling, begging, but he heard nothing.

Hineni saw his father's face, pleading with him to move. Baruch waved him forward and pulled and tugged, but Hineni stood firm.

Then he saw her. It was the blind woman he had noticed that afternoon across from the hotel.

Baruch stopped tugging at Hineni's arm when he noticed the boy's gaze fixed across the street. He followed the line of his stare and saw the old woman, sitting hunched in the gutter against the grimy wall of a building. She was facing Hineni and Hineni was staring back.

The woman opened her mouth and Baruch heard the sound of the stones gushing forth in all its beauty. It was more intense and louder than any single stone he had ever found. The woman closed her mouth and the sound stopped. The sides of her mouth turned up into a smile.

Hineni heard nothing. There was silence as thick as tar and as complete as the air around him.

Then it broke. He heard a single child's whisper as clear as if he and the child were the only ones in a sealed room. "Stop the guns," the voice said.

Hineni diverted his eyes from the woman to look for the child. There were many around but none were close enough for him to have heard such a soft voice. He heard it again. "Please, God, stop the guns."

The words repeated. Hineni continued to look for the child. The voice was still the only thing he could hear. It had not come from any particular direction, but from all around him. Then he saw a boy. Somehow he knew that the voice belonged to this child but he was not sure how he knew, or why he could hear him. The boy was leaning over a woman who was lying in the street thirty yards from Hineni. The woman's eyes were open wide and fixed at the sky. "Please, God, stop the guns," Hineni heard the plea again, yet the boy's mouth had not moved.

Baruch watched Hineni intently, forgetting for a moment the sound of the precious stone radiating from his sack.

Hineni walked slowly toward the boy. Then he heard another voice: "God, please help me," it said. It was a woman's voice, low and gravely -- an old woman who he spotted immediately. She was toothless and gray, with skin the color and texture of tree bark. She mumbled through her lips, which moved quickly but barely parted. Hineni heard her as clearly as if he had been thinking the words himself. He took a step toward her. He heard another voice; it was the old man from the lobby in the hotel and he, too, was asking for help. But wait, Hineni thought. That man didn't speak French. Nor, he assumed, did the others he was hearing now. Yet he heard them all. Understood them all. Another voice, and then another, and soon his head was swimming with voices.

"Father!" he called out.

Baruch was at his side.

"Do you hear them? Can you hear them?"

"The stones, Hineni? You can hear the stones?"

"The people. Can you hear the people? Can you hear their prayers?"

Then, instantly, Hineni heard it all -- not just those around him, but everyone who at that moment was praying. He understood all of them, individually and collectively, every word in every language. They filled him. Some asked for help. Some asked for peace. Some offered praise. They were everywhere, the voices. They all said the same thing. Not in words, but in essence. They all rang with the same Truth. The purity of Belief.

"Beautiful!" he said to himself.

Baruch turned to look for the old blind woman but she was gone. Hineni was nearly glowing. His eyes were shining and his face was lit up with happiness.

Hineni turned and gazed down the long street, out past the Tall Brothers, past the pavement, past the piers, and out over the sea. Baruch instinctively followed Hineni's gaze and stood to the side.

Hineni took a step forward. He felt nothing in his body. It was as if his entire body was comprised of the voices he heard.

Baruch heard his son's footstep crashing like an anvil dropped on the cobblestones. Hineni took another step, then another, and the ground shook in his wake, drawing the attention of those around him, despite the explosions. Hineni quickened his pace. In his mind, he was nearly floating; but to those around him, his footsteps crashed with a force that could decimate buildings. Hineni felt nothing. He was only joy and prayer. Now he was running. Faster and faster he ran toward the sea.

His eyes swelled and glowed. He neared the pier. He could see the French ships out in the distance. He ran to the edge of the dock and stepped off without slowing his stride. "Here I am," he thought. Then, as he leapt, reaching forward to eternity, he evaporated like a cloud of silver glitter. The stones fell silent.

Then the miracle happened. As Hineni leapt from the pier to become became part of the fabric of Truth and life, an angel, the hearer and conveyer of our prayers to a God who was also to fall silent, there was a calculation performed. The remaining time of Hineni's life, exactly sixty-two years, three months, ten days, one hour, eight minutes and twenty seven seconds, was divided among the people of the world, granting each nearly two more seconds of life. To each person, a gift was bestowed at the exact instant of Hineni's departure.

But the seconds were not added to the ends of their lives. No, they were granted right then, as if time were a piece of yarn being fed to a loom, which ran momentarily without unraveling the ball at the feet of the weaver.

A wounded soldier on a battlefield in Austria saw a bird flying overhead against the blue dome of the sky. A criminal in a Philadelphia prison took a deep breath inside his cell and let it out slowly. A small girl in Japan skipped a stone into the ocean, not knowing that a nearby volcano had just sent a monstrous wave to engulf her. An old man somewhere paused for a moment and savored his time.

CONFESSIONS OF A COPYCAT KILLER

J esus Christ was thirty-three when he died.

This is what I am thinking about when the suction cup that's holding my instructions to the bathroom wall loses its grip and falls into the bathtub. I watch it happen. The clear silicon gradually changes from a flat circle back to a cone and then plunges straight down into the water. It happens slowly enough for me to react, but for some reason, I am frozen and just watch, fully knowing the consequences. So, now I have to fish the thing out from where it landed, nestling under the ass of the woman in the tub. This is a real problem because her body keeps listing every time I take my hand off her, and I am struggling to keep her hair dry.

As I pull the instructions from the water I am cursing my stupidity. Not only was my suction cup too small to hold the instruction card to the wall, I also did a poor job laminating the card. Blue ink has snaked its way between the two loosely joined pieces of plastic. It looks like the packaging from a finished freezer pop with some residual juice creeping through the plastic. It's only by sheer luck that I have not started cutting yet, or else her blood would have seeped between the seams and mixed with the ink. I laugh sarcastically at my predicament, thinking, What would Jesus do?

It really drives me crazy. Every time I think I have my act together, I find that I've overlooked some detail. I know what the problem is: I just can't let myself trust my own togetherness. The more confident I become, the more inevitable my ensuing disappointment. There's always some unintentional smudge, a faulty knot, an over-enthusiastic knife-slash, or some other neglected, asinine little thing that could have been avoided -- if only I had maintained a state of constant anxiety. I wonder what the cops will think when they find traces of my carelessness this time. They'll think that I'm a clown: some schmuck who doesn't know how to buy the right suction cup or properly laminate an index card. If they only knew about my attention to detail. The meticulousness I employ to beat down my anxiety to a level so low a first-time mother wouldn't wake from it to see if her newborn is breathing at four o'clock in the morning. Damn. Sometimes it makes me want to cry.

The irony of my current situation is that I could have finished this job without the laminated instructions in the first place. I had, as always, completely memorized what to do. Not that I have a knack for memorization, like Mozart, who by the age of four was able to play long pieces of music perfectly from memory. It takes work for me to memorize. I have to come up with mnemonics. For example, Step 9 is Cheery English Ardently Love Boiled Potatoes, which stands for Cover Eyes After Laying in Bathtub Prone. I take the printed instructions simply because they give me some vague, reassuring sense of supervision, as though I'm not in this alone. It's like turning to a written recipe that you know by heart, which is a perfect example, actually, because I grew up watching my grandmother make her great grandmother's knishes from a recipe that she could recite in her sleep. Yet she would read the directions from her recipe book out loud, line by line, every Friday afternoon. Not only that, she would pre-measure each ingredient as if she were counting pennies to bring to the bank. She would flatten off a cup of sour cream with the back of a knife, creating a white circle with an edge so sharp that it looked like it had been carved with an engineer's compass. Then, when she got to the step that called for the sour cream, she would hold her sagging arm aloft, look at the recipe, and read out loud: "Add one full cup of sour cream to the smashed potatoes!" She'd drop the contents into the bowl, scoop the inside of the measuring cup clean with a rubber knife, then clean the knife itself with one index finger until she was absolutely certain that precisely one full cup of sour cream had been added to the knish filling.

They say that cooking is art and baking is science. Maybe that's true for chefs and bakers. But for most of us, they're both more like painting by the numbers. I wonder if it ever occurred to my grandmother that by changing the recipe just a little, she could have made it her own.

Of course, following directions is comforting because you don't have to think. Most people don't want to think. They just what to do what they're told, which is really what instructions and recipes do: they tell you what to do. Jesus, I am so pathetic. See... there's Jesus again.

I just caught sight of myself in the bathroom mirror. I look ridiculous with this puffy blue shower cap on my head, which keeps slipping down, practically resting on my eyelashes. I bought a box of them for work like this. They're too big, of course, because I'm an idiot with an odd-shaped head. I bought them to keep any hair from being left behind. Smart, I thought, except that I'm too dumb to check the size before I buy them and so I punish myself by wearing these instead of buying a box of smaller ones. I nudge it away from my eyes with my wrist.

God, what do I do about this ink in the tub? There has to be some clever remedy to remove or mask ink in water. I've heard that milk gets ink out of fabric, but milk in the water would be a bigger giveaway than traces of ink, and would hardly be according to plan.

What if, rather than trying to mask the ink in the water, I create an explanation for its presence? If she were clothed, I would slip a pen into her pocket. But she is not clothed. I have already removed her dress and laid it on her bed as if it were sleeping there (Step 4: Two-Star Generals Benefit from Dressing in Gowns). So she is now completely naked. Her hips are at water level and her dark, untrimmed pubic hair is just breaking the surface of the water like one of those fibrous plants that grow in shallow ponds. Her body is completely white, looking colder than it actually is. The temperate water is probably keeping her a little warm to the touch. At least, that's how it feels through my latex gloves. Her pasty skin certainly adds to her ghostly appearance.

This was a woman who hadn't seen the sun in years because she was always working. I followed her for two weeks. She worked in a mall at a gift shop, the kind that preys on vulnerable women who believe in an off-the-shelf notion of romance sold by way of satin and lace, scented candles and bath bombs. Not that there's even a hint of a relationship in her apartment. It's sad, really. The loneliness. The disappointment. And the thought that buying this stuff would make all that go away. She was thirty-three-years old.

That's why I was thinking about Jesus just before the suction cup malfunctioned. I recently turned thirty-three and for weeks I've been thinking about people who achieved greatness in their thirty-third year. There is no better way to remind yourself of your complete insignificance than to appraise the lives of successful people. Thomas Jefferson wrote the Declaration of Independence when he was thirty-three years old. Lewis Carroll wrote *Alice's Adventures in Wonderland.* Alexander Graham Bell created the American Telephone and Telegraph Company based on an invention he had created at an even younger age. At thirty-three he also patented the Photophone, a device to transmit sound on waves of light. Get that? Sound on waves of light! Maimonedes completed his work on the Mishnah. Michael Dell was worth $7 billion. And Orville Wright took off from Kitty Hawk (just shy of his birthday).

In fact, for every age through which I have passed I know the names of people who either achieved greatness or were well on their way to it by the time they hit that same age. And so far, no giant leaps for mankind have marked my life.

At twenty-four, Heisenberg proposed his renowned theory, and at thirty-one, he received a Nobel Prize for it. At twenty-four, Spinoza was expelled from the Amsterdam Synagogue for being a heretic, and at thirty-one, he published a work that improved on Descartes. Me? At twenty-four, I started to work for an accounting firm and at thirty-one, I quit that firm to join another one because their offices were fifteen minutes closer to my house and had better parking.

At twenty-two, Einstein published his general theory of relativity; Carl Linnaeus devised his system to catalog the world's plants and animals; Darwin set sail on the *Beagle*; Marconi got his patent for the radio; and I got an incomplete in economics because I forgot to write my name on my final-exam test booklet.

By eleven, Beethoven stopped taking music lessons because he couldn't find a teacher who could teach him something he didn't already know; Thomas Edison exhausted the usefulness of his local library, having finished, among all the other books, Gibbons' *The Rise and Fall of the Roman Empire*; and I smashed my balls into the handlebars of my bike when I rode smack into a parked El Dorado in an experiment to see if I could ride with no hands and my eyes closed.

So, at thirty-three, the same age at which Jesus was allegedly resurrecting the dead and himself, I purchased a goddamn suction cup not strong enough to hold a goddamn index card to a goddamn bathroom wall. Now, because of my idiocy, ink has seeped into the water and that's how they're going to determine that this wasn't the work of the real serial killer, but of a copycat killer.

Note that the term is *a* copycat killer; not *The* Copycat Killer. There is no *The* Copycat Killer. Although, if there was one, it would be me. I have killed twenty-two people, painstakingly reproducing the work of other serial killers around the country, and not once to my knowledge has anyone linked any two of my individual killings together. Of course, they always figure out that each was the work of a copycat. I usually end up with a blurb in a newspaper or a sound bite on TV. Anonymous and imperfect.

And those two components reveal the real masochism of impressionist killing, which is what I like to call it. If I were to do one reproduction perfectly, I'd get no credit at all. On the other hand, if I chose to make a name for myself, for example, by leaving behind some "signature" clue or writing a letter to a newspaper (a real temptation as I could select my own *nom de crime* before some eighteen-year-old newspaper intern decides to call me something patronizing and ridiculous like, "The Rerun Ripper"), I would be ceding that the perfect impressionist killing is unattainable. And I do not believe that is the case. I just think that I am too inept to pull it off. Like the ink in the water - - complete ineptitude.

Actually, I really have to deal with the ink so I can get out of here. I've decided to write on her index finger with a pen or marker so it looks like she just stained it writing. Then they can assume the ink in the water was just there because she had some on her hand. If there were to be a sizable investigation, I mean, if this woman were actually someone of importance, the medical examiner's office might figure out that the ink in the water and the ink on her hand were two different inks. But I highly doubt that the authorities would go to such trouble for a thirty-three year old sales clerk who smells like cranberry wax.

Another problem with impressionist killing is that even if I actually pulled off a perfect copy, I'd probably still be outed by the serial killer himself. Serial killers are like other self-important artists -- they don't like people doing their thing. Even the ones who avoid celebrity hate it when someone else steps in and grabs some of their fifteen minutes. In fact, there are several cases in which I was close enough to a flawless reproduction, or the cops sat so long on the copycat facts, that the real serial killer called me out as a counterfeit. One time I horned in on a widely publicized string of murders in Kansas. When the cops announced that a newly found victim (mine) had been linked to an earlier sequence of killings, the real serial killer wrote a letter to the *Kansan* that went to such lengths to prove the forgery that the details led to his capture. In three other cases involving my work, the real killers were so enraged when my work was lumped in with theirs that they upped their kill rate to reestablish themselves, got sloppy and got caught. It's funny. All told, I'll bet I save more lives than I take because I'm the catalyst that gets these guys caught.

Lucky for me, the reason detectives can't figure out that the same person is behind different impressionist killings is because there's no pattern among them, which is, of course, how they pin down a serial killer. I have no locale, no modus operandi, no victim profile. It doesn't take an FBI profiler with a PhD in criminal psychology and decades of experience to figure out that eight headless hookers tied to trees throughout Indiana is the work of one psychopath. But it would be nearly impossible for him to connect the sixth of those eight dead hookers to the fifth of nine fat women killed in Arkansas, who, like the others, was twenty-five, and left to rot in the trunk of her own car with various vulgarities written on her face in lipstick. (Orson Wells was still twenty-five when Citizen Kane premiered). To the different agents working those two cases, the copycat in Indiana had nothing to do with the one in Arkansas. Of course, complicating things for them is the fact that I'm not the only copycat. For example, while I did fat woman number five in Arkansas, it came out later that some other copycat had done fat woman number seven. And while I doubt that the other copycats are as woefully uncreative as me, and driven to make a career out of being a copycat, the fact that they exist sure does help to keep me under the radar.

I am now drying my hands on the towel that I brought with me. Actually, I dry my gloves. The towel is one of those blue, synthetic camping towels that are lightweight and powerfully absorbent. I use them because they do not leave fibers. Next, I hunt for a pen. I assume everyone has a pen handy in every room, like me. Not this woman. Not much to write down, I guess. Hopefully, I won't have to look too much further because the more I poke around the apartment, the more clues I'll leave.

Besides not having an obvious pattern, I also don't think I fit the serial killer profile. First off, I'm Jewish -- and truth be told, this is just not a line of work for Members of the Tribe. I date fairly regularly. I am not a loner. I am not impotent. I was not sexually abused as a kid. I am not sexually deviant. I never killed puppies or birds or shoved firecrackers into the rear ends of cats when I was growing up. I do have this recurring dream where a Catholic priest stands over my bed saying, "You're gay," and then he throws cold holy water on me. You think that might mean something? (Just kidding. I never dreamed that. I just felt like most memoirs have a too convenient and transparent dream revelation and was feeling a little left out.) My parents never beat me. They were boring and tried to do right by me. In fifth grade, my father brought a monkey to my class on career day. Not that he was a zoologist; but what kid wants to listen to a balding man talk for twenty minutes about being an accountant? I have no idea where he got the monkey.

All that said, my parents always seemed to be disappointed in me. I used to fantasize about one of them saying, "A ninety six in chemistry? That's fantastic. Let's go to dinner to celebrate." Instead I got, "A ninety six? Where are the other four points?" I was once scolded for my blood type being B plus and not "at least" A minus. Okay, just kidding about that.

This is not at all to draw a direct line between my parents' disappointment and the fact that I'm a serial killer. Though it occurs to me that if they did find out, it would be the criminal equivalent of finding out that I cheated on my SATs. "Bad enough you didn't know the answers, you had to get caught?" I may be an idiot, but I'm not so simpleminded as to seek their approval by killing people.

Speaking of incompetence, I can't find a single pen in the hallway outside the bathroom. No pens in the bedroom or the kitchen either. I figure it's typical of this kind of woman. Probably not too bright. Not only does she have little use for a pen, she obviously doesn't think them important enough to have around. I have to stay away from the windows as I look, which makes it harder. In the back of my mind I know that once I find a pen, I still have all the work to do on the body. I am such a moron.

So why am I a copycat instead of a regular serial killer? Because I couldn't come up with my own signature style. I'd had the urge to kill someone for a long time before I started, but I couldn't think of a unique way to do it. No method. Nothing jumped out at me. The first person I wanted to snuff out was a woman I knew from college -- I saw her three years after graduation. We were both in a trendy bar. I don't think she saw me. If she did, she didn't recognize me. Or worse, she saw me, recognized me and decided not to bother with me. I even gave her a little wave at one point -- nothing much, just a flick of my finger off the beer bottle I was holding. I think she saw it and just didn't bother. Afterwards, I was thinking, Man, I'd like to kill her. But no interesting way popped into my head. Everything I thought about doing was stupid and boring. Gee, maybe I'll just put her in a pit in the basement and make a dress out of her -- that's original. So in a way, she was saved by my lack of imagination.

After I balked at taking a few others for the same reason, I finally admitted I was not going to come up with anything good. The closest I ever came was an idea that was clever but impractical and, quite honestly, seemed too forced to be provocative, which didn't stop Pina Bausch, who was twenty eight when she choreographed her first work.

Here was my idea: I read somewhere about a paradox known as The Ship of Theseus. Theseus (who set out on his mythological journey to Athens at sixteen) was the legendary slayer of the Minotaur. The paradox is based on the assumption that Theseus' ship was able to survive long after he did because every time the old planks broke or decayed, they were replaced by new ones. If one board had been replaced, it would still be Theseus' ship. Two boards, three boards, five boards and a sail -- still his ship, right? But what if, over time, every single piece of the ship -- every board, sail, jib, rig, and so on -- had been replaced? Would it still be Theseus' ship, or a facsimile of it? And if it did cease to be his ship because all the original material has been gradually replaced, at what point did that transformation happen?

My idea was to use this paradox as my theme: If I killed two women, Amy and Jennifer, and placed them on two tables next to one another, then replaced Amy's right hand with Jennifer's right hand, Amy would still be Amy and Jennifer would still be Jennifer. Right hand and left arm. Right hand, left arm and a leg. Amy is still Amy, only with Jennifer's hand, arm and leg. But if I kept going, piece by piece, would Amy now be Jennifer? At what point in the exchange would the transformation happen? Fifty percent of the body? The torsos? The heads? I came up with another version where I would kill Amy plus several other women. First I swap Amy's right leg. Still Amy on the table. Then one by one, I trade her left leg, torso, head, right and left arms with the other women until all of Amy is replaced. Is the Frankenmonster on the table still Amy or a copy? When did it become a copy? Where is Amy?

It's stupid. I know.

And speaking of stupidity, I have completely botched this job. It is no longer just the ink in the water -- drawers have been rummaged through and there are footprints all over the bedroom rug. I'll have to get rid of these shoes once I leave. Given my carelessness, the cops won't even think it was an impressionist killer. When they walk into the apartment and find drawers rifled and footsteps throughout the house, they will immediately assume that it was a simpleminded attempt to make a routine robbery look like part of a string of serial killings to throw them off. It won't matter that her purse, television, and cheap jewelry are all still here. They will assume that something valuable is missing, even if they can't figure out what. And to think I once pictured my new career as an impressionist as the easy path. It was right around the time when I had finally given up on my paradox idea. Some guy started killing blond women in their trailer park homes near the Florida panhandle and Georgia, propping them up in sexually suggestive positions, without actually violating them (except, of course, for the killing part). It was elegantly simple. I thought, I could do that. Actually, what I thought was, I want to do that. Or, to be more precise, I wish I had thought of that. A life of mediocrity is an extraordinary thing to come to terms with. If I were completely honest with myself, I would say that I knew it would happen some day: that I would recognize my own mediocrity. I assume this realization comes to almost everyone (except those who actually do something). I just thought it would happen more gradually. For years, I dreamed about doing something great. But gradually, I came to realize that I was looking back on an unremarkable life that had been squandered. Talk about a profound transition. One moment you are a dreamer and the next, an apologist. You realize that some people are genetically programmed for greatness and you just aren't one of them. Crossing that divide is awesomely devastating, but it is also liberating. Once I knew that nothing I did would be of much consequence, I had license to do whatever I wanted because -- well -- in the grand scheme of everything, I just don't matter. No one cares; no one will even notice. I could stop pretending that people were watching me and waiting for my greatness to appear, because it was just not going to happen. Plus everyone else was already too busy worrying about their own significance or lack of it. So I decided to just get on with my pitiful, uncreative, plagiaristic butchery.

Sometimes I think of myself as a cover band, making a living off of other artists' creativity and success. Cover bands, oh, excuse me, tribute bands, must have tried so hard with their own songs before finally realizing that fame would forever be elusive. And you have to pay the bills. It's really quite pathetic. And it is what I do.

Of course the consequences of what I do are more serious than those of a cover band. The worst that can happen when you cover a song is a copyright lawsuit, whereas I am snuffing the lights of other human beings. I know they don't deserve it. But it's not like they were going to make any great contributions to this world. The cold truth is that an uneducated mega-store clerk with a pretentiously misspelled name like Tyffani is never going to be the next Michelangelo, who, by the age of 15, was under the patronage of Lorenzo the Magnificent, ruler of Florence. Pretty impressive. I know very well that Einstein worked in the patent office and that Bell had only a few years of formal education, but come on. Maybe it is a gift to her that she will never have to look back on her life through a lens of disappointment.

I go back to the bathroom to collect my things. It's over. I can't salvage anything from this job. I look at the woman. Her wide, empty eyes stare beyond me. I shake my head in disgust. I am so incompetent. This was her chance to be a part of something bigger. True, her untimely death was thrust upon her. But done properly, at least it would have meant something, if only to me. Now, it's nothing. I pick up my bag and scrutinize the bathroom one last time to make sure I'm not leaving a picture of me, my business card, and a map to my house. Idiot. I run out, leaving the job completely unfinished. They'll think it's a robbery. A stinking robbery. What a waste.

M'DOR L'DOR

Boeing Pinkhasov retreated behind a pillar atop the staircase just inside the Th13teen nightclub. He looked at his watch. It was two forty five. He needed to be in front of the main dining room at exactly four o'clock to lead his family inside for their grand entrance. He thought about all the guests who had assembled to celebrate his daughter Paige's Bat Mitzvah and groaned at the prospect of more than three hundred pairs of eyes focused on him. All he wanted was to go outside for a smoke and to be left alone.

He yanked the spotted handkerchief from his breast pocket and blotted his forehead. The fat white pillar provided just enough cover to steal a look at the hallway undisturbed. He surveyed the crowd of people slowly pouring in. He could name about three of them.

He thought about the day ahead. Only his wife Julia and Paige could cook up a Bat Mitzvah party so elaborate. He recalled his own Bar Mitzvah, twenty or so men in black suits crammed into the basement of a synagogue in Forest Hills. The only food was herring and black bread. The men got drunk on Slivovitz and spent the day clapping and stomping their feet. When they had exhausted their inventory of Jewish and *Juhuro* songs, they'd belted out anything that came to mind. They sang five rounds of "Come see the USA, in your Chevrolet," as if the

115

jingle had been a part of every Bar Mitzvah since the beginning of time.

He ought to start saving for Paige's sweet sixteen, he sighed to himself.

One of the caterer's assistants stood by the large interior doors on a low platform, barking out information about the many splendid rooms at the party. The guests flowed into the foyer like eager spectators at a sideshow, pausing at a table to pick up their seating cards and then clutching them as they walked in, as if they were show tickets or little treasure maps.

Boeing turned to the nearest bar station to order a drink. He opened his mouth to speak but stopped abruptly.

The bartender was tilting a bottle of wine over a woman's glass. Boeing saw enough of the label peeking through the man's fingers to recognize the distinctive, pear-shaped head of a bearded man with a tuft of hair on his crown. Boeing lunged forward and seized it.

It couldn't be.

It was a bottle of 1961 Château Pétrus Pomerol. Boeing had three bottles of it in his wine cellar, for which he had paid nearly forty thousand dollars at auction. This had to be one of those bottles. He smacked his forehead. Joey, the goddamn caterer, had been extorting so much money from him that Boeing had put himself in charge of the liquor supply for the party. Boeing had a cousin who knew a guy who knew a guy who got him a good deal. The delivery came to his home and he'd stored the alcohol for the party in his wine cellar. When the catering hands came to pick up the Bat Mitzvah booze, they must have grabbed the three precious bottles along with the rest of it.

Boeing reached over the bar and grabbed a glass. He poured the remaining gulp of Pétrus, swished it around and inhaled its bouquet deeply. It was rich. Thick. If only he knew more about wine. He really just hoarded the bottles for the sheer pleasure of seeing them shelved in his basement like rare books in a library. The three bottles of Pétrus had been his first purchase at an auction fifteen years ago -- a celebration of his first million. The bottles were a symbol. He had planned for the trophies to sit in his basement unopened forever.

He took a sip. He had to find the other two bottles. Ducking behind the bar, he searched through several cases of wine on the floor. No Pétrus.

The bartender was sure he had not opened another bottle with the same label. He said that the others could be behind any of the bars in the place because when they set up, the caterers had split up the cases of liquor to distribute them. There were thirteen separate rooms at the Th13teen, with at least one bar in each. Boeing slapped his forehead again. They had to throw such a party?

He stepped out from the behind the bar and set out for the next room. He saw a waiter with a white shirt and polka-dot bow tie heading toward him through the crowd with a silver hotbox strapped around his neck. Ah, yes. The Kobe Crescents, A.K.A. "pigs-in-a-blanket." He could not pass these up -- his mission would have to wait for just another moment.

When he and Julia had first sat down with the caterer, she preemptively vetoed Boeing's request for little pastry-dough hot dogs, saying they were low class. Boeing recalled that not only had he and Julia had them at their own wedding, but that she and his mother had sat up late the night before, cutting hotdogs into thirds and wrapping them in dough. Before he could raise the point, Joey suggested that the dogs be made from imported beef, introduced as Kobe Crescents, and accompanied by California wasabi dipping sauce. Julia accepted, on the condition that they go ahead with the vodka-soaked beluga caviar, which she knew Boeing was planning to reject.

So here were the scrumptious little piglets making their way toward him -- a proletariat coup.

Boeing placed two pups gingerly on a napkin and moved to a calmer corner of the room to savor them. He was anticipating the mouth-watering moment of ingestion when he heard a loud blast. From the corner of his eye, he caught what he thought was a fire breather disgorging a burst of flame from his mouth. He quickly realized that the fire was actually belched from one of the roasting stations that lined the walls. It had spewed its flame at just the right angle to make it appear as though it had come from the station chef's mouth.

Boeing looked down at fourteen dollars' worth of hot dogs lying at his feet.

He quickly checked to see if anyone was looking, then snatched one of the dogs as if he were plucking it from the clutches of a campfire. He popped it into his mouth, kicked the other dog under the bar, and set off for the next room to search for his wine bottles.

He chewed as he nudged his way through the guests. The hot dog was good -- real good. What a relief, after spending seven dollars a pop on these half-ounce portions of a mystical Japanese animal, slaughtered and stuffed into its own intestines nearly seven thousand miles away. But still, having felt as though he'd been kissed by the lips of God whenever he ate his mother's casserole, the caterer had simply let him down.

Interlude: The Story of Boeing's Mother's Casserole

Boeing could trace his lineage back to fourteenth century Dagestan through his mother's casserole. Literally. Until recently, he had no idea. According to a family legend his mother never told him (because it was reserved for daughters), it was in the remote mountain town of Kaitag, nearly seven hundred years ago, where one night, his greatest grandmother made a truly historic *bugleme* of lamb, carrots and onions. While usually able to forecast the exact amount her husband and two sons would eat, without leaving a crumb to feed the fruit flies that hovered in clouds over the refuse dumped in the town center, that evening, Boeing's greatest grandmother inadvertently cooked precisely seventeen percent more *bugleme* than was eaten. She was stunned when the men left the table and she was left staring at the uneaten portion in the bottom of the serving dish.

Not willing to waste a speck of food, she folded the leftovers into her *shashlyk tarki-tau* meat pie the following night. Her husband and sons said that it was, without question, the best *shashlyk tarki-tau* anyone had ever made. Yet when the men all stood to retire, exactly seventeen percent was left uneaten.

The next night, the *shashlyk tarki-tau* was mixed to fill *hinkal* dumplings. But the wise greatest grandmother made a smaller portion than usual -- about seventeen percent smaller -- figuring that her men would take charge and finish the meal. When the meal was over and the table vacated, exactly seventeen percent of her *hinkal* remained. The next night, she combined these leftovers with the ingredients for her famous fried *kouvyrdak*, adding fried onions to the leftovers. The family showered her with compliments after eating the *kouvyrdak*, but left exactly seventeen percent on their plates, with which she had to contend.

For days, she combined each preceding night's leftovers with the dish she was to prepare, whittling down the proportions daily, to no avail. After two weeks, she was serving a mere handful of food to her family, which they ate with great delight, leaving exactly seventeen percent night after night and, as one would expect, becoming quite obviously thinner.

Finally, rather than starve her family by reducing her meals to crumbs, she gave in to the enchanted food and increased the size more than two fold the following night. Then doubled it the following night. Then again, and again, until she was setting out a king's banquet before her family. Her husband and sons ate with great gusto -- crumbs flew, knifes cut, mouths consumed. In the end, exactly seventeen percent remained.

In time, she had a daughter. When the girl was old enough to help her cook, Boeing's greatest grandmother of leftovers showed her young apprentice the magic of the meals. Each night, no matter how much food she made -- whether enough to fill a thimble or a trough -- exactly seventeen percent was leftover when the table was cleared. Each subsequent night, the leftovers became part of the next meal. Every night, the family said the meal was the best ever.

The mystery was passed on. Her daughter cooked for years using ever-diminishing portions of that first portentous night's *bugleme*. Every night, seventeen percent of the greatest-meal-ever-served was left when the daughter's family went to bed. This daughter showed her daughter. That daughter showed her daughter. And so on, through the generations.

Until this one.

Paige had relayed the story to Boeing within just the past year. Having no daughter of her own, and with a daughter-in-law who, as the old joke goes, was only able to whip up reservations, Boeing's mother had asked Paige to the kitchen and told her about the leftovers while making that night's dinner. Paige ran to tell Boeing as soon as she was dismissed, accompanying the tale many times with exaggerated "uchs."

To Boeing, the story explained much about his mother's dinnertime behavior, and in particular, how warmly she would smile as everyone took their first bite of the evening. Boeing was also pleased (and even a bit surprised) that Paige had been respectful enough to listen to the old woman and save her cynicism for him. He suggested that she keep an open mind, since the only difference between the vampire stories she obviously chose to believe and her grandmother's tale were that the former had the benefit of having come to her via her friends and television.

Of course he dismissed the tale himself: in addition to the impossibility of seventeen percent of a meal being leftover no matter how much food was prepared, centuries of unbroken leftovers simply defied logistical odds. It would have been one thing for the royal chef at Buckingham Palace to claim that Her Majesty's shepherd's pie could be traced to a banquet set before Richard the Lionhearted. But if his mother's story was true, it meant that the meals had followed his ancestors -- Mountain Jews -- as they moved (or were chased) continuously across the vast Russian Caucuses and the Eurasian steppes throughout the centuries. He didn't know the details, but if he had been presented with them, would he believe that last night's casserole had been born in the highlands of Dagestan as a lamb *bugleme*, later relocated to Derbent as a *golubtsy* in a donkey cart, thenceforth carried to Krasnaya Sloboda in Azerbaijan as a *beshbarmak* in the bottom a rucksack, and then transported along river, over rock and through ravine to nearly every corner of the Caucuses? As if that were not impossible enough, could it be that after several centuries wandering around the steppes, the leftovers, by then in the form of Georgian *bazhe*, were hurried onto the plane (which his pregnant mother had named him after) and flown from Tbilisi to Istanbul, driven to Jerusalem, stowed away to London, and then smuggled in a small plastic bag in the bottom of a gray, water-stained suitcase to Pan Am's newly opened Worldport terminal in the recently renamed John F. Kennedy International Airport in the glorious state of New York?

So Boeing soon forgot about the story. That is, until his son and friends, in a fit of marijuana-induced starvation, snuck into Boeing's mother's refrigerator in the basement as she slept and devoured in minutes the seventeen percent remains of a beef stroganoff that had been set out earlier that evening. Boeing listened to his mother's spectacular, heart-breaking wails for weeks thereafter, and while he attended, he couldn't quite approve of the week-long *shiva* she solemnly sat for the empty casserole dish.

"You should have been a girl," was the last thing she said to him before she died two months later.

Boeing looked at his watch again. It was coming up on three o'clock. Guests greeted him as he walked through the party, praising the venue and the extravagance. They commented on Paige's performance. She had been absolutely wonderful. Boeing tried not to offend anyone as he brushed them off, but he feared he would get trapped in a conversation and waste precious moments during which another bottle of Pétrus could be uncorked.

He caught sight of Paige briefly as she passed with some friends to another room. Paige. Always in the center, ringed by friends. For a moment, he accepted the necessity of the grandiose party. To her, the Bat Mitzvah was about the celebration, not the passage. He just wished she would pause and reflect for a moment on the meaning. He had tried. He really had. But Julia, oh, how she had changed over the years. Boeing knew he was also to blame, of course -- buying forty thousand dollar bottles of wine -- but Julia had become all about the show.

He got stuck behind a waiter carrying a tray of sushi. The greedy crowd surrounded the waiter, boxing Boeing in. The waiter passed his hand over the tray to take a napkin and the food disappeared. Boeing's eyes popped. Now you see it, now you don't. Had anyone else seen that?

When the waiter brought his hand back over the tray, it was filled with empty glasses and plates. The waiter balanced the tray aloft with one hand, a small tower of glass and china above his head, and the crowd parted to let him through, eagerly awaiting the next concessionaire.

Boeing walked behind the waiter just as one would follow an ambulance in traffic. He passed a caricaturist who was sitting in one of the smaller rooms, busy lampooning the guests. He was drawing Boeing's aunt who had a protruding forehead and big ears. She seemed elated by the drawing although he knew she loathed her forehead and ears.

Boeing veered into a small room at the back of the nightclub. This little hideaway was dubbed the "Lipstick Room" for Paige's Bat Mitzvah. Several strawberry air fresheners hummed away in the corner, which gave the room the not-so-subtle ambiance of a taxi cab. The space was dripping with red velvet curtains. Fabric oozed down the walls and melted into big, fluffy, pincushion couches. Each couch had a large red button the size of cocktail plate sewn onto its seat. Mirrors hung at odd angles throughout the room, ensuring that guests could see multiple images of themselves from any spot. The floor was covered in thick, rubbery material that billowed as Boeing walked on it. On a large flat-screen TV, pictures of models in flamboyant outfits flickered, replacing the club's normal broadcast of soft-core porn. A disco ball and light fixture were set up behind shelves of decorative glasses, and they sent white spots circling around the room.

Two of Paige's friends, dressed in white sleeveless dresses, were perched on a sultry red couch. They looked like a pair of pearls resting on the tongue of an enormous clam.

A waiter circulated with a tray of hors d'oeuvres and a few glasses containing ruby-red wine.

Boeing recognized the wine. It was Antinori, selected to go with the lipstick theme because of its color.

Boeing beckoned one of Paige's friends over. The girl pushed herself up from the deep couch and then paused. She looked around the seductive red room as if seeing it for the first time -- as if it suddenly embodied all that she had ever heard about strangers and sex and perversion. She slowly approached Boeing without taking her eyes from him.

Boeing peeled a hundred dollar bill off the wad he had packed firm for the day and the girl stared at the money, perhaps wondering if it was a good time to run.

"At exactly four o'clock, you must be outside the main dining room," Boeing said. "If I'm not there yet, tell Paige that I'm on my way. Okay?"

The girl nodded.

Boeing turned and nearly ran from the room, but he tripped on the bouncy floor. He turned around and saw the wait staff and girls staring at him, unsmiling. He shook his head, regained his balance, and continued his journey through the Th13teen.

Soon he found himself on a balcony that overlooked the "CSI: Casino Room." Down below, he saw his wife Julia sashaying down the aisles between the card tables. She had on a short, tight, pink dress. Her rich brown hair was studded with pink pearls and her feet were bedazzled with a pair of pink sling-backs. From above, she looked like a majestic flamingo swimming gracefully through an archipelago of tiny green islands. She passed under a spotlight, which caught her just so, and the sparkle from her diamond ring flashed up at Boeing, who sighed deeply.

Julia, born and bred on the South Shore of the Isle of Long, he thought, as he descended the steps to the room. Boeing pushed through the guests and went behind the bar. The bartender approached, but was stopped short by Boeing, who warned him off with a look that could only be translated as, "I'm paying for this."

"Have you seen a bottle of Pétrus?" Boeing asked the bartender, who shrugged in response.

"Red wine, a pinkish tan label, picture of a monk on the front?" The bartender shook his head.

When Boeing finished rummaging through the bar, he went to the second bar in the room, and then the third.

Nothing.

He made his way to the stairs. A man and woman in their mid-sixties assailed Boeing as he mounted the final step out of the casino room.

"Boeing," the woman said, "Paige was marvelous." The man at her side nodded furiously.

"We're very proud of her," Boeing said, trailing off. He was momentarily distracted by two men with legs about seven feet long standing in a corner. When he turned to study them, he realized that they were just two roustabouts on ladders, fixing a garland that had fallen from a canopy.

"We hardly noticed the teleprompter," the woman said.

"Well, we hoped you wouldn't."

"There's no more *po'e* at the back station in the Tahiti room," the man said. Boeing was stumped for a moment, but then he remembered the Tahitian fruit concoction on Joey's menu list. Who were all these guests, sucking down *po'e*? He looked at his watch. Forty minutes. He leaned into the man. "I'll get there right now and find out what's happening."

"Well, I didn't mean for..." the man said, but Boeing was already gone.

As he walked away, Boeing wondered if the woman was being sarcastic about the teleprompter. After all, it was not really a teleprompter -- it was more like a Torah karaoke machine. Paige had scarce time to practice reading Torah. The poor girl had been so busy helping Julia plan the party. She had been integral -- integral -- in deciding everything from napkin colors to the shape of the balloons. She had to give the stationers handwriting samples to create a font for the thank you cards, which would be sent out using a database of the gifts received. She even helped Julia concoct the party's title: "Paige's Thirteen Favorite Things." Julia and Paige both thought that having only one theme was too limiting. So Julia suggested having a different theme in each of the thirteen rooms in the club, which, coincidentally, dovetailed nicely with the whole thirteen-year-old Bat Mitzvah thing, even if Bat Mitzvahs were technically for twelve-year-olds.

Paige had secluded herself in her room for half a day. She meditated on her life, consulted friends, and looked through magazines. Finally, she emerged from her retreat with a list of the thirteen things she loved the most in the world:

Chocolate
Strawberry lipstick
Cocktail umbrellas in coconuts
Tan feet
Muffin (her little white Bichon Frise)
Jacuzzis
Street artists
CSI
Clouds
Skittles
Sweatshirts
Skiing
Broadway shows

Boeing thought he was going to cry when she read it to them. Such simple things could make her so happy? He had fought Julia about the expense of the Bat Mitzvah until then. He had thought the extravagance was a waste and that the meaning of the day was getting lost. But at that moment, all he wished for was to protect his baby girl from the world, surrounding her with clouds and Skittles. If that meant a lavish Bat Mitzvah with thirteen rooms of silliness, so be it.

"Can we substitute back rubs for Jacuzzis?" Julia said, already scribbling ideas concerning how each room would be arranged and what it would contain.

Boeing had twenty minutes to get to the dining room.

He scoured the Tahiti room, a theme created around a drink with an umbrella. Polynesian drums pounded away through speakers. Most people were drinking the raspberry daiquiris served in coconut shells and topped with little umbrellas. There were large glass basins of the unctuous, red liquid around the room. Boeing looked under the grass-skirted bar tables and found nothing. He sat down in one of the white chaise lounges and put his head in his hands. A monkey scampered across the floor past his feet, pausing for just a moment to play with his shoelaces before darting off.

"Everything, okay, dad?"

Boeing raised his head and split his fingers to see his son Jeydyn, whose face was covered in a spiraling henna tattoo.

Boeing laughed. "You look like a freak."

"I'm not the one who thought, gee, if we have coconuts with umbrellas, we should have a Tahiti room. And what's Tahiti without tattoos?" He took a sip of his drink. His lips and mouth were stained from the blood-red liquid.

His boy. How fashionable he and Julia thought they were being: a *J* name and a misspelling -- double cool. Children as accessories. Somehow Jeydyn had survived it. He was so even-keeled. Nature over nurture.

"I lost my bottles of Pétrus," Boeing said, almost embarrassed. A lot of things seemed silly just then. "And you're too young to drink."

"That blows," Jeydyn said and took another sip. "Oh, and hey, there's no more *po'e* at station three."

"You're very wise," Boeing said and stood up. He bestowed a kiss on his son's head. "Enjoy yourself," he said and walked out.

Boeing had ten minutes to get to the dining room. The lights had started flickering throughout the club to let people know it was time for the main event. The crowd flowed toward the dining room. Boeing drifted along with it until he came upon the "Cloud Room" and went inside.

Two industrial fog machines were working mightily to ensure that the room was filled with a thick gray mist. There was a slow, dull, melodic soundtrack playing, which sounded like a digitally engineered calliope. The muted rhythm seemed to be carried in the fog itself, permeating it and giving it a sense of weight. A strobe light flashed somewhere in the room, giving Boeing the feeling that he was lost in a storm. If he remembered correctly, someplace in front of him, another bartender was mixing up revolting combinations of milk, fruit juice and liquor and serving drinks with names like "white cloud," "silver cloud" and "thundercloud." The strobe went off again and Boeing hunched his shoulders reflexively.

A long red balloon expanded from the fog in front of his face and then disappeared. There was squeaking -- rubber being bent and twisted. The balloon was suddenly thrust back to him in the shape of a dog. Boeing pushed it aside.

"Where's the bar?" he asked.

"To your left," said the balloon man. The strobe flashed.

He reached the bar, which was skirted with white ruffles. "What can I get you?" a voice said.

"I'm looking for a bottle of wine. It's a red wine. It has a pinkish tan label with a picture of a monk on it."

Boeing heard bottles clinking. "I think I saw..." the voice said. "Ah, here it is."

A bottle appeared in front of him with the waiter's hand wrapped tightly around the neck. The face of the monk nearly glowed. He took the bottle. It was empty.

"Any more like it?" Boeing asked solemnly.

"Nope. That was a good one. People drank it down in a few seconds."

A few seconds.

Boeing found the girl he had given a hundred dollars to waiting outside the dining room as instructed. He was about five minutes late.

"Did they go in?"

The girl shook her head. "Didn't see Paige."

"Thanks," Boeing said, and dismissed her. She looked much younger than she had in the Lipstick Room. She was small. Thin. The seductive room had unfairly added a decade of time and a heap of unearned sexual experience upon her. As she walked away, the thought crossed his mind that men -- old men like him -- might look at his Paige the same way. He quickly blotted out the thought, shaking his head and turning to a painting on the wall. The last bottle must be in the dining room, he thought. The painting depicted a man and child, both sitting on a floor, which seemed to be covered in sawdust. The child was playing with a big top as the man watched over him. He could not make out the painter's name from his signature. It could have been priceless or worthless, which is how he viewed most paintings. He wondered for a moment about the painter. Was he dead? Was he painting something at that moment? Was he making lunch? Talking on the phone? On the toilet? Out with friends? Walking in a park? Strange how their two worlds were linked at that moment through his work, and only Boeing knew about it. It was like reading an out-of-print book, knowing that you might be the one person in the world reading that book at that moment -- a special connection to the author. Now and then, Boeing meditated on the thought of his great grandfather and speculated how he might have spent a particular day in his life a hundred years ago. Who he spoke to. Where he walked. Whether he ever stopped to think of his own great grandfather or the great grandson who was thinking of him now. One day, after Boeing was long gone, some great grandson might wonder about him. What was Boeing leaving him?

Suddenly, he heard an elephant blasting its trunk on the other side of the dining room door. He realized it was just the band starting up. He looked at his watch. It was ten after four. No Paige and no Julia.

Finally, Paige came walking toward him. Boeing stared at her, remembering a video he had taken years ago. Paige on a swing in the backyard, her soft hair billowing out each time she came toward him. She had been wearing a little denim dress with a yellow flower embroidered onto her chest. They'd had an argument that morning over socks. He wanted her to wear warm ones. She wanted the thin ones with ruffles. She always won. He taught her to pump her legs and dared her to swing higher with each pass.

Now she was walking toward him in a white wedding dress that had been altered for the occasion. Julia swore they had combed New York for a simple dress but found nothing. Then she'd had the brilliant idea to check out Vera Wang, just for inspiration, of course. One thing led to another and three thousand dollars later, Paige was wearing a much-altered wedding dress to her Bat Mitzvah. Boeing knew what Julia was up to -- she might as well have printed the purchase price right on the invitations.

Paige's thick brown hair was sprinkled with pearls and pulled back in a tight twist. Her face was the same as the girl in the video. Sweet. Round. Soft. She was carrying Muffin, who was enduring a pink bow clipped to her head for the day. The dog yelped and Paige set her on the floor. Muffin scampered to Boeing's feet and sniffed at his shoes. His little girl was officially a woman today. Chocolate. Lipstick. Tiaras. Clouds. Women never outgrow their toys either, do they? He had to work to keep his tears from falling. Boeing opened his arms to welcome his princess.

"Where the fuck is Julia?" Paige said, stopping short of his embrace to take a sip of her Appletini.

Boeing lowered his arms slowly. "I'm sure she'll be here in a minute." He paused. "You shouldn't be drinking," he added meekly. Two nights prior, he and Julia had discussed whether their children could have a drink at the party. He said no, Julia told him to lighten up. All teenagers drink, she said, reminding him they did when they were teenagers.

Joey popped his head out of the main dining room to see if everyone was together. "We're waiting for my mother," Paige said. The caterer rolled his eyes and slipped back into the room.

"Joey," Boeing called after him. But he was gone. "What a clown," he said softly.

"F-F-S, Boeing, for fuck's sake, she doesn't give a good god damn shit about today. Doesn't she know how important this is? Dammit." Paige rubbed her temples and took another sip from her drink.

Boeing weighed the comment for a moment.

"This may be your day, Paige, but..." He stopped and walked over to her. It was hard to picture her now as that little girl on the swing. He took the drink from her hand, placing it gently on a low table near the door.

"Jeesh, sorry. I was just saying," she said and looked past Boeing. "Julia!" Paige yelled. "Where have you been? They're about to get started. "

"Sorry guys, I ran into Aunt Vera. We ran out of *po'e* in the Tahiti room."

Joey peaked out and saw the three together. "Excellent," he said. "Okay. Now what's the password?"

No one smiled.

"Just a little joke. So serious. I'm going to open the door in about one minute. Please be ready."

Paige blew a long stream of air from her lips and shook her head. Julia hunched over her cell phone and typed a text message, which went off with a satisfying ba-bleep. She adjusted her dress, hoisting it up for a second to pull a non-existent fold from her stocking. Her phone ba-leeped back and she smirked.

Boeing put his hands into his pockets, walked to the wall, and stared at the painting again.

"Julia," he said, without turning around. "Do you remember the night before our wedding? Cooking with my mother and arranging those flowers for the tables?"

"What?" Julia said, typing into her phone.

"I asked..."

She looked up. "Yeah, yeah. And?"

He turned around. There was a long silence as he and Julia held each other's eyes. Paige stared in between them, as if focused on a line that connected them for a moment, then nervously bounced her eyes between them.

"You're embarrassing me. Uch."

The door cracked open and a man came out carrying a clarinet, followed by a man with a trumpet, followed by a man with a tom-tom. Each time Boeing thought the door was closing for good, another musician propped it open and slipped out. Finally, they were surrounded by a troupe of ten tall performers, all wearing brightly colored patchwork coats. Paige's Torah portion had been *Vayeishev*, in which Joseph receives his coat of many colors. Broadway shows had been on the list of Paige's favorite things. It all just came together: waiters with Technicolor Dreamcoats in the main dining room. Perfect.

The thumping music came to a sudden stop. Julia moved to one side of Paige and Boeing the other. They tangled their arms together.

"Ladies and Gentlemen, boys and girls," they heard the bandmaster say on the other side of the door. "Please direct your attention to the main entrance of the dining room." There was a short drum roll. "Please put your hands together and join me in a warm welcome for the world's greatest, utmost tremendous, most splendatious, Bat Mitzvah in the world... your host and hostess... and the woman of the day... Paige Pinkhasov." The doors swung open and the muted roar suddenly burst upon them. The musicians struck up a klezmer version of "Any Dream Will Do" and acrobats entered the darkness like gladiators entering a coliseum.

Boeing, Julia and Page clasped their hands and raised them up high. They were quickly swept onto the dance floor by their guests. Boeing could barely make out the faces as they blurred past him. The lights were still out. Spotlights followed the family, while other beams swept the floor. Boeing's uncle grabbed him and spun him around. Jeydyn appeared and danced with his father for a moment. A small group of guests hoisted Paige up in a chair and bobbed her up and down. Then a group lifted Julia in a chair and a spotlight shown on her. Her dress was bursting with countless sparkles in Boeing's eyes.

Then he was pushed backward. He thought he was going to fall when he realized that a chair had been slipped under him. A group of men crouched around. With a loud groan, they heaved him into the air. He looked down at the crowd from the best seats in the house.

Paige's friends, the boys, were all jumping wildly to the music below him. They reached toward Boeing from the darkness as they jumped, trying to tap him on the hand or the arm. They were getting fantastic height, as if leaping from springboards. Two boys jumped with their arms around each other, as though they were permanently connected at the waist. Another boy juggled napkins. Suddenly, a spotlight hit Jeydyn as he was thrust into the air.

The music clamored as the family Pinkhasov swung above the crowd. Someone passed a table cloth to them, which they held above the people's heads like a tent. Green glow-sticks appeared. As each wand was cracked, it bathed another face in a phosphorescent hue.

When the song changed, Boeing and his family were lowered to the ground. The bandmaster raised his arms and then brought them down slowly, with a loud shush into his microphone. The crowd calmed and he had them form a large ring. The spotlight was tempered.

"Will Paige and Mr. Pinkhasov please step forward," the bandmaster asked softly. He wore a top hat and tails, with a red glittering cummerbund and bowtie. He had a thick, waxed handlebar mustache. Everyone took a step back. Boeing hesitated when Paige pulled him forward, saying "F-F-S, Boeing, let's go," she said, with an impish grin.

The musicians floated into *Sunshine of My Life* and the guests let out a gelatinous awwwww.

Boeing took his daughter's hand and held her close. She nestled her head into his neck and they rocked slowly. The cheesy smiles of his guests surrounded him, but none as cheesy as that of the bandmaster. Had he hired that guy?

The song ended, the guests applauded. "Ladies and gentlemen, please direct your attention back to your tables, where a bever of vegetation awaits your phytophagous palates. That means, your salads are ready."

Boeing screwed up his eyes.

The guests slowly retreated into the darkened dining room, using their glow sticks to illuminate their paths, looking like fireflies dancing in a field. Boeing stood in the front of the room with Paige.

"Now, ladies and gentlemen," said the bandmaster, "it's not routine for me to yield the floor to anyone, but I'll ask you to please direct your attention to my favorite abliguritist, that is, the man who threw this fantabulous party, Mr. Boeing Pinkhasov."

Boeing took the microphone and cleared his throat. The room got quiet, save for a few pieces of cutlery clinking against plates.

"When I was a little boy," Boeing started, "maybe six or seven, I found a cocoon in my backyard. Every day that spring, I watched it. Hour after hour. I built a little hut for it out of a shoebox to protect it from the rain, which I decorated with drawings of butterflies and flowers. I would lean in real close and blow on the cocoon ever so softly to comfort the butterfly with the warmth of my breath.

"One afternoon, my mother took me to town to buy some groceries. We were gone maybe an hour tops. When we got back, I ran to the yard to check on my cocoon and stopped short. It had split open and the butterfly had flown away. I was devastated.

"I cried and cursed at the trees and the sky and the sun. I kicked and tore the shoebox to pieces. Since then, I've carried around a feeling of having missed out on something, and the feeling that life -- and all its beauty -- was passing me by when I wasn't looking.

"Then Paige was born and as I sat watching her in her bassinet, day after day, hour after hour, I swore to myself that I would never go for groceries. I attended every moment of her life. And finally, this day, this day of her Bat Mitzvah, I'm watching my beautiful little butterfly emerge and it's the best day of my life."

The guests were silent, savoring the vision of little Boeing Pinkhasov and his cocoon shoebox. Those who knew him felt that they understood him better and those that didn't wished they did.

The lights in the room brightened a bit, and Boeing looked at the bandmaster. The man smiled broadly at him from underneath his handlebar mustache. The band struck up a few chords of dinner music and the bandmaster walked over to Boeing to retrieve his microphone. "That was the best one I've ever heard," he said.

"Every once in a while, I get it right," Boeing said.

He started to hand the microphone to the bandmaster, but then took it back.

"One more thing," Boeing said, loudly. "Please be on the lookout for a bottle of wine with a tan, pinkish, label with a picture of a balding monk on the front. A hundred bucks to anyone who finds it. Thank you."

THE OBSERVER EFFECT

Sasho found the bulk of his mother's documents before he had opened the drawer to her old desk. She had tucked her passport, Bulgarian Communist Party card and wedding papers into a kitchen cabinet and wrapped them in a thin plastic grocery bag with a single piece of tape across the front reading, "Death Papers."

The heavy secretary had been in his mother's bedroom for as long as he could remember. More than 60 years. He was forbidden to touch it as a child. Not that there was any reason to, except, of course, for the prohibition.

Above the desk was a bookcase holding the Russians and Hristo Botev, the one Bulgarian poet whose work everyone in the country could recite by heart. There was a French book that displayed musical instruments. When he was a child, his mother would take it down on special occasions. It had illustrations of the strangest instruments -- things he imagined sounding like angry elephants or blasts of bus exhaust. Flipping through its weary pages now, he realized for the first time that it was just a mail catalogue.

The desk had a flat wooden slider separating the drawers below from the shelves above. It flipped down like a drawbridge and the panel served as a writing table. There were slots and small drawers behind the panel.

In his youth, he had imagined that this mysterious piece of furniture contained magical gifts and secrets; one drawer held an endless supply of gold coins and one of the slots was a secret window through which he could watch people he knew going about their business. How he could use those coins now that capitalism had come to save them.

And the magic slot? He would have used it to spy on Slava Nikova, the girl who lived in an adjacent bloc.

He was surprised by the fear that swelled in him as he touched the edge of the slider. With his mother gone, the desk was his. But the fear was there all the same, as well as a foreboding sense of disappointment. There would be no coins and no magic window.

He pulled the slider down. Just behind the hinge was a silver pen engraved with his grandfather's initials. He found several stamps and considered their value. They were certainly old, but he knew enough to deem them worthless.

Tucked into one of the slots was a black leather *yarmulke* that must have belonged to his father. It was permanently creased, having been folded for so long. How long had it sat like that? His father had died when he was just two years old.

He opened a small envelope drawer, pulling gently on its cold, glass knob -- a sensation he would remember with near perfection for years to come. The drawer was held together by dovetails without a drop of glue, made before the imports from Romania had appeared with their aluminum tracks and ball bearings. There were three beads of resin along the drawer's top edge. He withdrew the packet of yellowed pages folded neatly inside, releasing a scent of time. Dust. Decay.

The pages were light and almost translucent. The sheets, about twelve in all, had been folded into thirds. He slowly unfolded them. There was writing on both sides.

"Dearest son," the letter began. His aging eyes and his mother's diminutive handwriting forced him to hold the pages at arm's length.

The overwritten story was typical of his mother's narrative style. After reading the first line, which asked him to recall the rise of Tito, he was sure that somewhere deep within the twelve-page, double-sided treatise was a point.

After a two-page recounting of Yugoslavian leader Tito's view of communism and his split with Stalin, his mother told a story about his father's employer.

His father had been an engineer in a plant outside Sofia and had enjoyed a close relationship with the director. The director, in turn, had relationships with several suspected Bulgarian Titoists. These relationships were too much for the Cominform, and the director and his wife had disappeared in the summer of 1949.

At this point, Sasho's mother reminded her son of the risks Bulgaria had taken on behalf of its Jews during World War II. Bulgaria had sided with the Nazis; part of a geopolitical gamble involving Greece, Macedonia, Romania and the Treaty of Neuilly. But even at the highest levels of government, Bulgarians had set out to ensure that no Bulgarian Jew would fall victim to German hatred. Everyone knew how, beyond earshot of her Nazi escorts, Queen Giovanna had whispered to a foreign ambassador over a case of jewels at an exhibition in Sofia that she was in desperate need of visas and passports.

"And because of this," Sasho's mother wrote, "when it was our turn, we set out to save the families of those who had saved ours. Regrettably, my dear, I let the first part of your life pass thinking you were too young for the truth. And then, when I thought you were old enough, I sensed the right time had passed."

The truth?

Several paragraphs later, after a babbling section about a mother's love, she wrote, "We loved you as if you were our own." He stared at the page.

He had been adopted.

Identifying his birth parents turned out to be surprisingly easy. Sasho went to the Central State Archives and found the name of the plant director assigned during the time his adopted father had worked there. Then he consulted one of his father's surviving friends for more information. The friend reminisced for a while about the man Sasho had always thought was his father, and then Sasho asked about the director. The man fell silent and his eyes slowly worked their way around the shape of Sasho's face. Sasho noted the exact instant the man figured it out.

"It was not an affair," Sasho said.

"That is obvious," the man said. "You look like your birth mother."

About a month after Sasho's discovery, he sat and watched his wife, Tatiana, washing the dishes after dinner. Thick and stout, she wore a brown frock that was tightly cinched around her waist. Sasho held a bottle of stiff *rakiya* in one hand and a glass of soda water in the other. It was Friday night and he always permitted himself a few extra drinks on Fridays to unwind from his week. It was not by definition a strict Sabbath observance, but it had become his way of letting go of the week.

His mind wandered as he watched his wife scouring pans with her strong arms. Her head bobbed as she talked about their youngest grandson being sick. He heard her say something about sending the boy some candy and a few puzzles.

She still didn't know what Sasho had learned and the thought of articulating the word "adoption" to her made the ordeal too real to contemplate.

She had lit two Shabbat candles earlier, which sat on the windowsill and eventually started to flicker as they burned down to the end of their wicks. One of them sputtered and died. It took a moment for the acrid scent of burned wax to reach Sasho's nostrils.

He clenched the bottle. He was not a Jew. His birth parents were Christian -- Eastern Orthodox. But how was this possible? So much of who he believed himself to be was defined by his being born a Jew. He had always believed he could feel the difference, that something in his blood made him different, something inherited that was more than mere genetics. But now he knew that this sensation was built on an illusion. His connection to an ancient tribe was nothing more than a figment of his imagination. But shouldn't that feeling have vanished when he learned the truth? He had no Jewish blood in his veins, yet he still felt something.

He imagined taking all the things that had once made him feel like a Jew, made him feel different, and putting them into the palm of his hand. That way, he could hold them to his face and observe them closely. What were these things? How were they changing now that he was looking? He was struck by a sensation similar to the one he got when he couldn't reconcile his name with who he was. It's all *gluposti*, he thought suddenly -- bullshit.

Tatiana placed the last dish in the drying rack, shut off the water and wiped her hands. She gazed at him for some time while his eyes remained fixed on the bottle. Her soft face had aged poorly; her wrinkles reminded Sasho of the old women in the mountains whose faces were creased and grooved. But her eyes were fresh and young. Deep and warm.

He drew a breath. "I was just wondering about what it means to feel like a Jew," he said before she asked.

She laughed. "If you are thinking of converting, let's please do so before Passover." She kissed his head. "Do you want company?"

"No."

"Then please don't be long," she said, and went to bed.

He started to think about conversion. What a strange concept. Certainly there are rituals, but how easy it is. People flit from god to god like children regrouping among friends in a schoolyard. And nobody trusts a convert anyway. He's like a Bulgarian who finds work in France, and roots for the Parisian football team against Sofia. The biggest farce was surely forced conversion. What did it mean to be forced to convert? History had shown that a suppressed religion survives like a flower bulb in a winter of hatred, waiting to sprout in a spring of enlightenment, and to flourish in a summer of tolerance. No, there was no real test of faith, except maybe death.

Sasho stood up slowly and felt the blood rush from his head. He sat back down and laughed. He had always been a terrible drinker -- another gift, he had thought, from his lineage. He tried again, slowly. He took his glass to the sink and rinsed it out, placing it upside down in the dish rack. He was a good husband, he thought, and went to bed.

The next morning, he woke up to the smell of *banitza*. He could almost dissect the separate aromas of layered pastry dough, butter and goat cheese. There would be apricot jelly and toast. Dark, thick coffee. He dressed quickly and went to the kitchen.

"You're already dressed," Tatiana said, placing a fragrant dish of apricot jelly in front of him.

"I'm going for a walk, maybe to Synagogue."

She stopped, then gently put a hand on his shoulder and squeezed it lightly. "Your mother was a good woman. We all miss her."

He put his hand on hers. Her eyes were there to greet him and they held each others' gaze for some time. He assured her that he was just feeling a bit down, but that all was well.

They ate breakfast together in silence.

Sasho went to Synagogue, which was crowded with a group of Israelis in town to help build an electronics factory. After services, he hurried off to the Jewish Community Center, which was in a small square dotted with thin skeletons of trees and lined with crumbling cars, mostly old Ladas.

He greeted the Center guard and showed him his passport.

The entrance hall was dimly lit and quiet. He walked into the main office and looked around. In the center of the room was a chipboard desk, its veneer curling up several inches at each edge. Two metal chairs faced the desk and a black office chair was set behind it. The room was completely filled with books. The desk and all three chairs were stacked high with heavy volumes. There was a long shelf behind the desk that covered the entire wall and overflowed with books. From under a stack somewhere, a phone rang.

After a moment, a young man came into the room. He gave Sasho a quick tap on his shoulder and a smile. The phone continued to ring. "*Stiga!*" the man said -- enough. He stared at it as it continued, bulging his eyes each time it went silent, as if daring it to ring again. Finally, it stopped and he sighed. "Who calls a Jewish Center on Shabbat?" he said in flawless Bulgarian, which always amazed Sasho since the young director was a foreigner -- an American. Andrew Weiner.

Andrew cleared off a chair and invited Sasho to sit down.

Sasho looked at Andrew. He had been sent by one of the international Jewish organizations, and Sasho had come to him several times with questions about the holidays. They rotated in and out, these young helpers, every two or three years. They came ostensibly to help build a vibrant Jewish community, and they probably believed in their mission to some extent, but Sasho also suspected they were drawn by a romanticized vision to come-of-age in post-communist Eastern Europe -- like in a number of Western novels that were sometimes laughed at in the Bulgarian press.

Andrew was something special, though. The others behaved as though they had superior knowledge to bestow upon an ignorant community. Andrew spent more time asking questions than dispensing opinions.

"I'm not a Jew," Sasho blurted out.

Andrew did not move, which left him leaning forward with his mouth half open. There was a moment of silence.

"Do you mean you don't want to be a Jew?"

Sasho assured him that he hadn't misunderstood. Andrew wrinkled his brow. "Times are hard in Bulgaria. People come here claiming to be Jews all the time. We send their kids to school. We help some move to Israel. But I don't understand. You are coming to tell me you are *not* a Jew?"

Sasho told his story, describing the letter, Tito, his father's boss, the company friend. When he finished, Sasho turned away. "I have always felt like a Jew. I still feel like a Jew. But yet I don't."

Andrew gave Sasho a moment. Then he asked if he had any of his original documents -- perhaps adoption papers, or something from a rabbi? Sasho did not.

"Well, then," Andrew said, "let's have a look." He climbed onto his chair and reached for several books that were scattered across the highest shelves. He passed them to his visitor. Jumping down, he rummaged through the tomes he'd selected, his finger running down the Hebrew text as if he were tracing the course of a winding river on a map. It was somehow comforting to Sasho that a book was needed to answer his questions, as though the old sages had expected him to come on this day, to have this problem, and to need their guidance.

"Hmm," Andrew said. "The general answer is that you are a Jew. You were raised a Jew, you identify as a Jew. Everyone in this city knows you as a Jew. You even come to synagogue... sometimes," he laughed. "You are a Jew as far as we are concerned."

"Yes, but my blood?"

"There's a more technical answer. It can't change your blood, but it may change the way you feel. You know that there are many groups of Jews. These groups recognize each other differently, particularly when it comes to conversion. So if you want to be acknowledged as a Jew among all Jews, you might consider going through an Orthodox conversion. It would be on record with the Jewish counsel -- the *Bet Din*."

The word "conversion" sounded to Sasho like the clap of wooden blocks. "Conversion? But you said I am a Jew."

The young man's faced softened. "Think of it as a reaffirmation. I told you, the most important thing is that you identify as a Jew. But there is an Orthodox process and three requirements you must fulfill. You have to affirm your intention to live by the laws of Judaism. You have to have a proper circumcision."

"But I had one."

Andrew nodded thoughtfully. "Very interesting. You're adoptive parents may have done this. You found no papers from a rabbi?"

Sasho said no.

"It's unlikely that in Bulgaria you had a circumcision for any reason other than a *bris*. But if you want to be sure it's kosher, you can have a *hatafat dam brit*, which means a 'taking of a drop of blood.' Believe me, you are very lucky.

"And the third requirement is a ritual bath -- the *mikvah*. But the most important part is the first -- your intention to live a Jewish life, which you already do."

Sasho asked if his family would have to know.

"Only if you want them to. You may want them there if it would give the day more meaning. That's up to you."

"No. This is for me only. And you will not tell anyone."

"Well, we need to speak to the rabbi, and he will get the witnesses and a *mohel*. The *mohel* is the one who will perform the *hatafat dam brit*. But that's it."

Sasho considered the growing circle of insiders. "Too many people will know. I don't want all these people in town to know this about me."

Andrew paused for some time. "I have an idea."

Two weeks later, the two men were on a train bound for Bucharest. It wasn't ideal. Sasho would have liked to have had the ceremony in the large Moorish synagogue in the center of Sofia. He loved that old brick and stone structure. He often wondered how something so Jewish could survive in Eastern Europe. It was a place that filled him with pride as a Bulgarian and as a Jew. But going to Romania was better -- less sentimental, but more secluded.

He had expected trouble getting a Romanian visa, but Andrew and the Bucharest rabbi were able to arrange things with a letter and a small "facilitation fee." The only hard part about the trip was lying to Tatiana about it.

"I didn't tell my wife," Sasho said to Andrew. He looked out the window. A shepherd's flock was scattered across the green landscape.

"Why not?" Andrew asked.

Sasho shrugged. "It is complicated."

"What did you tell her?"

"That you suggested I come with you to some meeting and that I didn't understand what it was about, which is true, in a general way."

Andrew laughed. He had arranged for his organization back in the U.S. to sponsor the cost of the train and hotel, so at least Sasho didn't have to use his own money and therefore have to explain the expense to Tatiana.

The Bucharest rabbi met them at the station. He was American and Sasho was relieved to see he wasn't like some of the rabbis that came through Sofia, the ones that were just a little older than some of his grandchildren.

They got into the rabbi's car. He was chatty, and alternated between English and Hebrew. Andrew translated. They spoke mostly about American football.

They drove to the Bucharest Great Synagogue. As they walked to the building, the rabbi gave a history of the synagogue and the Jews in Romania. Sasho nodded politely, but barely listened. He was taking in the building's façade. Not as nice as the one in Sofia, but it would do. They entered the main sanctuary and Sasho looked up at the synagogue's high arches and gilded accents. It was beautiful. How wonderful to conduct the ritual here.

They walked around for a while, with the rabbi giving them a private tour.

"Let's go," the rabbi said abruptly in English, and headed toward the exit.

"Aren't we doing it here?" Sasho asked.

Andrew translated for the rabbi.

"No, no," the rabbi said, shaking his head. "This is a museum now."

Andrew watched Sasho's expression drop. "Museum" is a word that sounds the same in almost every language and didn't need translation.

As they reached the car, Sasho turned around one last time and then got in.

When they got to the rabbi's office, the rabbi sat back in his chair and put his feet up on the desk. He said something to Andrew in Hebrew.

"The *mohel* is meeting us here," Andrew translated.

"How are you feeling?" the rabbi asked.

"Good," Sasho shrugged.

"Do you have any questions?"

"No." Sasho turned to Andrew. "Did you tell him my story?"

"Only what you wanted me to," he replied. Andrew said something to the rabbi, who gave a deep nod and an earnest look that Sasho could only describe as not smiling. Sasho wanted the rabbi to know he was not converting in hopes of a handout. He was a Jew and this was just a formality.

There was a knock on the door and a small man with a black-and-gray beard entered before the rabbi could invite him in. He wore a light spring jacket and was damp with sweat.

"Is this the man?" the *mohel* asked in Hebrew.

Andrew nodded eagerly.

The *mohel* looked at his watch and then to the rabbi. "Okay, let's start." He took a small black box from inside his jacket pocket and set it on the table. The rabbi leaned into the hallway and called two more men into the office. Andrew explained they were the witnesses. The office suddenly felt warm and crowded.

The *mohel* turned to Sasho. "*Baruch ha-ba b'shem Adonai...*"

"Blessed are you who comes in God's name," Andrew translated into Bulgarian as the *mohel* continued. "Blessed are you Adonai our God, Ruler of the Universe, Who sanctifies us with commandments and commands us regarding the circumcision of the convert."

"Take down your pants," the *mohel* said.

"Wait a moment," Andrew said. "This is very fast." He asked Sasho if he was alright.

Sasho nodded but his face flushed. He started to take his pants off and the *mohel* stopped him by leaning forward and grabbing his hand.

"That's far enough." The *mohel* opened the box and withdrew a needle from a small plastic envelope.

Sasho looked away as the *mohel* gave him a swift poke, producing a small drop of blood. The *mohel* handed Sasho a gauze pad and then took a small clear vial from the black box and held it near Sasho's face.

"Smell it," Andrew said.

Sasho breathed in the strong, pleasing scent of cracked cloves.

"It's a reminder of the sweetness of Jewish life," Andrew said.

The *mohel* continued. "*Baruch atah Adonai, Eloheinu melech ha-olam, shehehiyanu, vekiamanu, vehigianu lazman hazeh. Mazel tov,*" the *mohel* said. "Blessed are you Adonai our God, Ruler of the Universe, for giving us life, for sustaining us, for enabling us to reach this day. *Mazel tov.*"

The *mohel* took Sasho's hand and shook it without looking at him. Then he waved to the rabbi and walked out. The two witnesses each murmured *mazel tov* to Sasho and left. Sasho finished buttoning his pants.

"*Mazel tov, mazel tov,*" Andrew said and threw his arms around Sasho. Sasho gave him a slight smile.

The rabbi stood up and pulled a large book from a shelf. He put his hands on Sasho's shoulders and guided him towards the book. He spoke and Andrew translated.

"This is the section of the bible where the covenant between God and Abraham was forged. It says that when Abraham was ninety-nine years old, Hashem appeared to him and said, 'Walk in My ways and be blameless. I will establish My covenant between Me and you, and I will make you exceedingly numerous.'" They continued reading and Sasho listened closely, feeling little connection to the first man to have crossed this same boundary.

The rabbi excused himself. Andrew looked at Sasho, who was looking out the window.

"I'm sorry," he said. "I didn't expect it to be so rushed."

Sasho shrugged.

The rabbi then returned with a bottle of *tzvika*, and they toasted Sasho and life.

They stayed at the Intercontinental hotel. Sasho had never been in such a nice place before. With Andrew's organization paying for such accommodations, no wonder Bulgarians discovered Jewish grandmothers all the time.

For a moment he wished Tatiana had come so she could have seen the room, but he flinched at the thought of her having witnessed the minute-long ceremony.

That little bit of sorcery made him more Jewish? He groaned. On the contrary, it only further diminished the sense of exceptionality he had once felt, and reinforced the notion that his faith had been merely self deception. *"Gluposti,"* he mumbled. Perhaps the way to feel more Jewish was to stop scrutinizing it so closely.

The thought of going home before the rituals were completed crossed his mind many times that night. He could knock on Andrew's door and say goodbye, but he didn't want to see the disappointment in the young man's earnest face. He could just go back to Sofia on a night train and never speak to Andrew again. But what good would that do? No, he would have to keep going with a process that was no longer meaningful to him. Maybe the *mikva* would be the answer. Maybe after he completed all three steps he would feel differently. He doubted it. Still, there was always some satisfaction in being right, no matter how awful the truth.

The rabbi picked them up the next morning and they drove to the *mikvah*, which was in the basement of a school. Several boys walked out as the three men entered. Just before they exited, the boys swiped off their *yarmulkes* and stuffed them into their pockets. Sasho watched them walk away and become just another group of kids. Romanians weren't as good to their Jews as the Bulgarians were, he remembered.

They descended a flight of steps and entered the *mikvah* area, a gloomy place with cinderblock walls, tiled floors and florescent lighting -- hardly what Sasho expected from a holy place of ritual purification.

Andrew translated the rabbi's instructions. Sasho was to go through a doorway, remove his clothing, take a shower, and return. The rabbi handed Sasho a white terrycloth robe, unfurling it with some flourish.

"It's a gift," Andrew said, "to remind you of the purity of this moment."

In the back, Sasho took off his pants and shirt. He moved slowly and deliberately. The smell of mildew filled his nose. He removed his underwear and socks and stood naked in front of a full-length mirror. If only he had not opened that drawer. He thought of Tatiana and of seeing her the next day. He would be a real Jew for the first time, recognized by some far-away group of rabbis. He decided he would tell her, suddenly needing her to know.

When Sasho returned, Andrew and the rabbi were with two other men -- the witnesses, Andrew explained, young scholars. Sasho shook their hands with as much poise as a mostly naked man could. He sat down opposite them all on a bench, aware of his pale, bare knees sticking out from beneath the robe. He ran his hand over his chest several times, smoothing out creases that weren't really there.

Andrew explained that the three men, including the rabbi, would serve as judges to ensure that Sasho was voluntarily accepting the commandments.

"Are you converting of your own free will?" the rabbi asked.

Andrew translated, adding that the word conversion was a technicality and that Sasho was, as they had discussed, just reaffirming his love of Judaism.

"Yes."

"Will you raise your children as Jews?"

Sasho laughed when the question was translated. "They already are. But I promise if there are any others, they will be Jews as well."

"Do you recognize Hashem as the one and only God?"

Sasho hesitated for just a second. "Yes."

The rabbi had said, "recognize" and not "believe in." This, Sasho thought, was very clever. While he was not sure he could affirm his belief, he was certainly willing to recognize *Hashem* over any other god he could think of.

"Do you accept the obligation to observe the *mitzvot*?"

"Yes."

The rabbi then motioned for them all to go into the *mikvah* room. There was an aluminum railing just inside the doorway, leading to a tiled, sunken tub the size of a large table. Sasho walked down the stairs and into the water. It was just barely warm. Uninspiring.

He stepped to the center of the pool as instructed and stood for a moment with just his head above the water.

Repeat after the rabbi, Andrew instructed.

"*Shema Yisrael Adonai Elohenu Adonai Echad.*"

Sasho repeated the familiar words slowly and carefully. The rabbi gave him a signal and he went under the water, ducking low to ensure his entire body was submerged. He raised his feet from the floor and floated for a moment to enjoy the peaceful sensation of weightlessness. Then he brought his feet back down to touch the floor. He slowly straightened his legs and let his head break the surface of the water. Emerging with his eyes still closed, he noticed the water felt warmer as it gave way to the cooler air above. He listened to the water dripping into the pool and echoing in the small room. He ran his hands over his head, forcing the water from his hair down his back. Opening his eyes, he gazed up at the florescent lights above. One of the bulbs had blown and needed to be replaced. He frowned.

Sasho remembered Abraham, who had also once straddled two worlds. He hoped that something truly wonderful transpired when the ninety-nine-year-old man emerged on the other side of the covenant, and that whatever he had first looked upon after his great transformation had made him deeply and thoroughly happy.

But he wondered.

THE REASSIGNMENT OF NUMBER 0021681

Something flashed and 0021681 realized he was no longer standing in front of the house. In front of him was now a towering olivewood door. To his left and right were thousands of cubicles, within each sat a Wheel of Fire.

"Uh oh," he said to himself.

0021681 approached the door. It was covered in Nubian gold, and studded with Balas rubies, mined from under the mountain Syghinan. It had scattered circles of lapis lazuli, each whose pyrite inclusions sparkled like a universe of tiny stars. It was carved with scenes of the ceaseless battles of the Kings, and its gem encrusted stiles magnified the light emanating from 0021681's eye sockets. The entire space was awash in a glow known only in eternity.

In the center of the door was a small black and white plate that read, "Director, Office of Divine Resources." 0021681 took a deep breath and exhaled a stream of white-hot fire that licked and curled in eddies up the front of the door.

He knocked.

He was beckoned in with words that sounded as though they were sung in the voice of the multitudes. 0021681 entered and the door closed behind him.

The sole figure in the room was draped in the same linen garment as 0021681, and his loins were also girded with the same fine gold of Uphaz. He sat on a golden chair in the shape of an eagle, its wings reaching out to the sides. The desk in front of him was a sea that stretched out as far as 0021681 could see, and the forms and computer screen on top of it rose and fell on monstrous waves. The room was ablaze from the fire of their eyes and the lightning that was their faces.

"How've you been?" asked the director, without looking up from some paperwork.

"Can't complain," replied 0021681. "Blessed be He."

"Mmm," said the director, who squared the forms he was reviewing on the watery desk in front of him and laid them down. He motioned to 0021681 to come further into the room. "You know why you're here, I assume."

0021681 glowed slightly brighter.

"And?"

"And what?"

"And what do you have to say for yourself?"

0021681 dimmed slightly. He looked beyond the director, out into the light that filled the void behind him. He shrugged. "I did what I thought was right."

"You what?"

"I did what I thought--"

"Who asked you to think?"

That was the problem, 0021681 thought. He could not help but think, especially when he was set on not thinking. The more he tried not to think, the more he thought. He was thinking at that very moment -- thinking about not thinking -- and he knew the director knew it.

"You have but one mission. Have you forgotten it?"

"No, but--"

"But, nothing." The director lifted a piece of paper, which glowed with his touch as if it had been dropped into a pit of fire, yet it didn't burn. "This is your job description," he said, waving the paper at 0021681. "Expectations of the Bad Escorting Angels." He looked up. "That's you."

"You don't have to read that to me," 0021681 said.

"Oh, but I think I do," said the director and he cleared his throat, which sounded like the song of a million nightingales resounding through the valley of Mount Hira. "The mission of the Bad Escorting Angel is to accompany every man in his charge home from synagogue each Shabbat with his partner -- the Good Angel. If, when the Angels arrive at the homes of their charges, the candles are lit, the challah is on the table, etcetera, etcetera, the Good Angel says, 'May it be thus next Shabbat.' Then the Bad Angel -- that's you -- must respond, 'Amen.' If the Angels do not find the house thus, the Bad Angel -- again, that's you -- says, 'May it be thus next Shabbat' and the Good Angel must respond 'Amen.' Pretty straightforward, wouldn't you say?"

This was 0021681's first encounter with any of the upper ones in the Office of Devine Resources, those inhabitants of heaven in charge of monitoring angelic performance and allocating glorious tasks based on His requests. In front of him was the director of the department -- a solid line in the organizational chart to Him. The lower dominions in the ODR were mostly responsible for ensuring that forms were complete and for rolling out new programs each Jubilee year, which usually coincided with the busy seasons. Most were paper pushers, rumored too have failed at just about every other Angelic role. There was a saying, "Those who can't do -- Minister. Those who can't Minister -- work in ODR." The director, however, was rumored to be at least as intelligent as the cherub who wields the flaming sword at the entrance to the Garden of Eden, which was not saying all that much, but it was something. He was also rumored to be what the humans call an asshole (a word that may have been man's greatest gift to Heaven).

The director continued. "You have but one simple task. Say 'Amen' when things are thus, and say 'Let it be so next Shabbat' when they are not. That's all you need to be concerned about. Nothing about thinking."

0021681 recalled the moment earlier, just before he was summoned to the director. He and his partner, the Good

Escorting Angel, stood shoulder to shoulder, just like the angles carved into King Solomon's temple. The Good Escorting Angel had just finished his blessing. Things had been thus -- as always -- at the house of the man they had escorted home from synagogue. The table was set, the linens were crisp and clean, the challah was covered and the wine was generously poured. And as always, 0021681 could hear the faint sound of crying coming from a back room. The wife of the man, huddled in a corner of the bedroom, fearful and in pain. Each teardrop that fell from her eyes sounded to 0021681 like the forsaken prayers of Job.

0021681 felt a nudge. "Ahem," the Good Escorting Angel said, waiting for 0021681's response to his prayer. The woman moaned as the husband entered the house in front of them. It was at that moment that 0021681 decided it should not to be thus next week. Then he was here.

0021681 twinkled briefly. "Exalted One," he said. "It is true that the home was thus. But the man's wife was in the bedroom with a bloody nose and bruises on her arms and chest because he had beaten her."

"I don't think you understand."

"I do understand. It was thus every week. How could I call that upon her each week just because the silver shines in the home? Surely this is not what He meant for Shabbat."

"It isn't up to you. It's set forth in our policy and procedures, which you received on your first day. You have to fulfill your mission. In fact, you are nothing without your mission. You are your mission. If every Angel decided to act on his own, there would be chaos, and that is no way to run things.

"You remember how we all cried at the destruction of the Temple and how we wept when Abraham tied Isaac? The skies filled with our sorrow. I could have smote the soldiers who destroyed the Temple with less effort than it takes me to remove a hangnail and unbound Isaac with nothing but a snort. Did I? No. It is He who decides these things and it is so. When was the last time you read our Organizational Mission Statement?"

"Torah?"

"No," the director grunted, sounding like a thousand cape buffalo thundering across the Savannah. "Doesn't anyone read the mission statement? Do you know how many millennia we spent writing that thing?" He pointed to a sign on a flaming wall a hundred miles away. "Mission Statement: Do, Then Obey."

"Yeah, well..."

"'Do, Then Obey.' Simple. Your actions are unprecedented."

"It's not unprecedented. What about the Angels who revealed the destruction of Sodom to Lot and his wife? They disobeyed."

"And they were exiled for a hundred and thirty eight years. But even so, they didn't disobey. They screwed up. There's a difference. Angels screw up all the time. Remember the Angel who gave Daniel that convoluted metaphor about rams and horns? The Holy One, blessed be He, had to send Gabriel to straighten it out."

"What about, you know... Them? They disobey all the time."

The director laughed, and the laugh roared like the waves that had pounded Noah's ark.

"Them? You are not one of Them. They have Free Will. You are one of us. He made Them like Him for Him. He made us like us to service Him and Them. That is our role -- we are what They call 'glorified gofers.' We get our missions and They feel the wrath of them." He paused. "Don't you love the way They depict us descending from the clouds, sun shining, horns of light. Wings. Always wings. If more of Them actually read the Word, They'd know that when we come to visit, it's with fire and fury on our breath. Do you remember Balaam's face?" The director laughed again, which echoed through the sky like the seventh blast of the trumpets outside the walls of Jericho.

"If we don't matter, what about what They sing in *Shalom Alechem*? You know, *'Bar'chuni l'shalom, malachei hashalom.* Bless me, O ministering angels.' They ask us to bless Them. I hear it every week."

The director slammed his fist into the sea in front of him, splitting it asunder. *'Bar'chuni l'shalom* has nothing to do with you. If They interpret it that way, They are sorely mistaken. It is a request to Him and you are simply there to administer it at His behest. They can sing and pray all they want to us, but it's up to Him what is granted. He is mightily jealous and He doesn't want us taking credit for His work."

"Then why bother. Why does He even need us?"

"He doesn't need us -- They do. He created us for Them. He defines us by our missions. He defines Them by their potential. That is why He gave Them both free will and feeble brains. With just one or the other, there would be no challenge, no quest. But since They can't wrap those puny little brains around the idea of Him, He gave Them something more their speed to help them along -- us. He knows that without us to send them signs and deliver His messages, They would turn to idolatry. I mean, really. They witnessed with Their own pathetic little eyes how He wrought the plagues upon Egypt, split the Red Sea in two, made manna fall from the sky, and then Moses turns his back for a minute and They're on their knees in front of a golden calf? Come on. They can be so stupid sometimes.

"And He didn't grant us free will for the same reason. Imagine what it would be like if you could personally consider their prayers. 'Oh angels,'" he whined, "'grant us peace, heal my mother, smote that airline attendant.' They'd worship you quicker than the golden calf. It's bad enough They put us on coffee mugs. He hates that."

"So He does need us."

"Okay, so He needs us. But you know what I mean. You are nothing but an instrument, a channel, an intermediary. You don't even have a name."

"I have a number."

"That's for internal use only."

"Here's the thing," 0021681 said. "I don't think I want to be part of an organization that values candles and challah more than what they represent."

"You don't have a choice. We're the only game in town. And our policy is--"

"Then maybe it's time to change policy. You said yourself that you cried when He bound Isaac. You knew it was wrong, we all knew it was wrong. Yet we did nothing. We need a grievance policy or something. We need a way to let Him know we don't always agree with what He does. If we band together--"

"Are you kidding? A union?"

"I hadn't thought about it that way. But yes, a union. The Divine Brotherhood of Angels. We could have a say in the missions. And if He won't change policy, He'll have to do His own dirty work. I'm not going to bless the house of a wife beater ever again."

"That's for sure. And thank you for the perfect lead in. You're being reassigned."

"Reassigned?"

"Better than exiled."

"But--"

"You're being placed in the Throne room. Chreubim."

"Cherubim?" 0021681 said. "That's not a reassignment, it's a demotion."

The director shrugged, which whipped the cold winds up the face of Mount Ephraim.

"Come on. You can't agree with that decision? I did what I thought was a good deed. I prevented a woman from being beaten every Shabbat for the rest of her life. Somehow that doesn't fit with organizational policy? Doesn't that bother you?"

"It wouldn't matter if it did. That's exactly the point. I do, then I obey. Even asking me to question His judgment is dangerous ground."

"And that doesn't bother you either?"

"I do, then I obey."

"You're a robot."

"It wouldn't matter if it did bother me."

"They should put you in a call center in the lower world. You'd be perfect."

"That is His will, not mine. And it is time for you to go," he said and 0021681 disappeared from the office.

The director took out a yellow sheet of paper and a pen. His mission was complete. Now, the paperwork.

One week later, 0021681 sat in the throne room between several Angels, each with the face of a man, the face of a lion, the face of an ox and the face of an eagle. They sang together, "Holy, holy, holy, is the Lord of hosts; the whole world is full of His glory."

0021681 sang too. He could not resist. The throne room -- something about the throne room -- quieted his thinking. The words poured forth with rapture.

Then he felt the Holy One, blessed be He, with him. He felt closer than He had ever felt, closer than in all the millennia of 0021681's memory.

Then He guided 0021681 from the throne room, down through the sky of the lower world, across the treetops, to the home of his former charge. 0021681 passed through the front door to the dining room with Him. The table was set. The challah was covered and the cups of wine were poured. It was thus. 0021681 heard the woman's soft voice in the bedroom and he entered. She was crying. But not from fear or sadness, but from happiness and relief. Her husband, strong and healthy as he was, had died that morning for no apparent reason. And she was safe.

BAAL-TSHUVA

On a Friday afternoon, John Adler launched up the stairs, taking three at a time. He reached the fourth floor and barged through the stairwell door into the hallway, digging for his house keys.

That Rabbi is a gift. New guy. Few months. Four, maybe?

He slid the key in the lock.

Stuck. A trick. Push, lift, pull, turn.

A bead of sweat slid from between his shoulder blades and down his back to his waistband. He kissed his fingertips and touched them to the *mezuzah*. He entered his apartment, taking in the warm, moist smell of stewed meat and parsley.

John loved the frenzy of his Friday afternoons, typically barreling into Shabbat like a harried runner across a finish line. He took his time at the office on Fridays before leaving, finding trivial activities to occupy him -- recapturing the desktop from the week's documents, wiping down the computer screen, topping off the stapler -- meaningless tasks that promised the rest of the afternoon would be filled with kinetic energy.

First a dash to the subway, then off to the vegetable vendor, the grocery store, and the liquor store for wine. Home for a moment then off to *shul*. He liked to think of it as an ancient weekly ritual, transplanted to the Upper West Side of Manhattan. It made his Shabbat all the sweeter. Made him feel a part of it.

He looked at the clock: *7:19. Too late.* He had to miss *shul* this week. *Kabbalat Shabbat.* Welcome Sabbath. The apartment was filled with summer heat. *Dammit. The air conditioner. Too late.* He opened the window, which fell back down on his thumb. He snapped his hand back, instinctively putting his thumb into his mouth. *Stupid.* He looked at it. *Black for sure.* It throbbed. *She'll notice.* Naomi. *Disgusting. She's at shul now. Dinner's not ready. Band-Aids. Cover it.*

He piled five plates, gathered settings and glasses, and placed them all on the dining room table. Then he returned to the kitchen to check on the crock-pot which held a brisket, steeping in its juice.

A crock-pot with a timer. Always a loophole.

He shook his hand in the air. It still throbbed.

He set the table and continued to get ready until someone called from the doorway. John came out, wiping his hands on a dishtowel. He opened the door to Naomi and her brother Oren.

Naomi said, "We missed you at *shul.*"

Hair down. Wavy. He liked the way it framed her heart-shaped face. *Lipstick. Perfume. Cinnamon?* John watched her mouth form her words. He loved the way her tongue rode her lips when she spoke. *A baby's lisp. Sally sells sea shells. She misthed me?*

"I had a lot to do here," he said. *Four guests. Traditional meal. Everything just so.* He leaned in and kissed Naomi's cheek. He thought she turned slightly toward him so that he grazed the side of her mouth. "Come in. Sit down."

Oren walked into the living room. "Jesus, John. Could you turn the heat up in here? I'm boiling."

Not funny. "Sorry about that. I forgot to turn on the air conditioner before sundown." *Notice? No electricity after sundown.* "I have a friend who lives next door. She'd be happy to come in and turn it on." *Shabbes goy.*

"Is she hot?" Oren asked.

"Not really."

"Forget it. I'll just open more windows."

John squeezed his sore thumb into his palm. *Still hurts.*

Neal arrived.

"Come on in."

Neal introduced his latest girlfriend, Julie.

Finally Julie. Not-so-Jewish Julie. Nice nose. Freckles. Roots a bit dark. Renee Zellweger? A Catholic school girl, for sure. No tartan skirt? Knee socks. Mmmmm.

"We brought you some *cha*-lah bread," Julie said.

John winced. His mother used to say *cha*-lah bread, like "chat," instead of challah, with that soft and guttural *H*. She would shimmy back and forth on the few Friday nights a year his parents decided to "have" Shabbat, singing, "Cha-cha-cha, cha-cha-cha-lah bread." *Have Shabbat.*

He took the loaves and turned them right-side up to read the wrappers. *Kosher. Pareve.*

"Don't be so obvious, John," Neal said.

"I was just..."

Julie looked at Neal.

"Forget it. John's a big flamer."

"Oh," Julie said. She turned back to John, offering an overly pleasant smile.

"I'm not gay," John said.

Neal laughed. "He a flaming *Baal-Tshuva.*"

Very funny.

Julie looked confused. *Cha-lah bread wouldn't know what Baal-Tshuva meant.*

"I grew up reform," John said. "A real bacon-and-eggs-on-Saturday-morning Jew. About five years ago, when my uncle died, I started to learn more about Judaism." *Too much information.* "*Baal-Tshuva* means returnee." *Sounds like being born again. It's not.*

"Me, too," Julie said. "But I only started since I met Neal."

Jewish? How stupid.

Neal laughed, reading John's look.

"Don't worry, I get it all the time," Julie said.

"Me, too," John said. *Love the look on people's face when they find out.* "Anyway, dinner's ready, come in and sit."

Neal introduced Julie to Oren and Naomi and they gathered around the table. John asked Oren if he would say the *Kiddush.*

Oren poured wine into the shiny silver *kiddush* cup and raised it. He paused for a second to examine the large Star of David embossed on its side and then looked down and noticed the four smaller matching cups on the table.

Thank you. John had spent half a paycheck on the set a month before. They weren't exactly the impetus for hosting Naomi, Oren, and Neal, who had magnificent Jewish upbringings and had him over for Shabbat meals with some frequency, but rather they gave him the courage to do so. Oren began to sing the prayer, as he always did, with unabashed intensity. *My house, Oren's Kiddush.* John glanced at Naomi. Suddenly the cups seemed silly.

John had learned to sing certain prayers, parroting Hebrew he mostly didn't understand and didn't really care to. *In English, they're like religious greeting cards.* Sure there was a sense of tradition, but he really just did it so he could sing along with the others -- to participate and blend in. He envied how Oren and Neal could lead *benching* after dinner or walk into any *shul* in the world and not have to ask for page numbers or fear being called on for an *aliyah.* He knew parroting didn't trick anyone. It was obvious who was comfortable and who wasn't. He had tried to imitate Oren's cadence and intonation -- even feigning boredom sometimes as he sang -- but it never sounded right. The new cups didn't help, either. It was just too late. *An imposter.*

Oren poured wine from his cup into the small ones and passed them around. *A waste. Oren's cups are old. They have a story. A great grandfather. A boat. A sack. These gleam. Advertisements. Proxies for tradition. Future heirlooms. The first annual.* John drank his wine quickly and collected the others as soon as they were placed on the table. No one complimented him on them.

"Anyone who wants to wash, come to the kitchen," John said.

John handed a towel to Neal, who gave it to Julie as she finished washing her hands. Then he reminded her to be quiet until after the blessing on the bread with a light touch of his finger to her lips. *Intimate.*

They returned to the table. John pointed to Julie, silently asking her if she wanted to say the blessing. *Not nice.* Julie shrugged. Neal lifted the challah loaves and said the prayer.

John recalled his first real Shabbat observance. It was on campus his freshman year with Hillel, the organization that provides programming for Jewish students. He had gone with his roommate who'd told him, "Best meal on campus." *Better than Ramen.* He remembered listening to the wine being blessed with the full *kiddush*, then washing, and the private embarrassment of never having heard the full prayer before and not knowing that washing was part of the Shabbat ritual. *Thought learning a bunch of prayers and not eating* treyf *would be enough. So stupid.* That year he had also discovered that there was a second half of the Passover Seder -- *after the dinner?* How could his parents have left this out? *Cha-lah. John with an h? Why not Christopher? Chris. Christ. Christ follower. John the Disciple.*

John brought out gefilte fish, each slice resting neatly on a white plate with a wedge of carrot and a leaf of romaine lettuce. *Tradition. Not grandma's plates, though. First annual.* He slipped his bandaged thumb under Julie's plate as he placed it on the table in front of her. *Carpenter's hands. John with an h.*

"I never had gefilte fish like this before," Julie said after a bite.

"Raised on fish in a jar, huh?" John said.

"Yeah."

"Me too. This one is actually good, right?"

"Comes frozen," Oren said.

Not everyone's grandmother grounded her own carp.

Oren was saying something.

Julie. Jew-lee. John figured she wouldn't know that you can't eat fish and meat from the same plate. *No way. Hurry up so I can say it. Should have made smaller pieces to speed this up. Too small is so* goyish. *Why? Never hungry at Kevin's house; always smelled like stew. Catholic. Maybe just WASPs starve you. Mom's food was white bread with mayonnaise. Fried baloney. Mayo. English muffin. That was good.*

How about some mustard in the house? What kind of Jews don't have mustard? For the refrigerator door at least? Like the empty mezuzah. They didn't know it wasn't supposed to be empty. Claph? Claaf? What's it? Finally everyone's done. "Let me clear the plates before I bring in the meat. Anyone need water?"

"How archaic," Oren said.

John turned and looked at him. *Here it comes.*

"Oren," Naomi said sharply.

"It may be archaic," Neal said, "But it's still *halacha*." He turned to Julie. "Religious law."

"Actually, medical *halacha*," Oren said, raising his glass to his lips. He looked out over the tilted rim for a moment, waiting for everyone's attention, then he put the glass down. "Bet you don't know where it comes from."

"Oh, please tell us, Rebbe Oren," Naomi said.

John cleared his throat. *Contribution. Finally.* He had read about it on the Internet. The question was being served up, just as he had hoped. *Oren, my straight man.* "You eat fish and meat separately so you don't get confused and accidentally choke on a fish bone. That's not really medical *halacha*, it's more like, you know, thoughtful."

"Baaaaah!" Oren said. "Common misunderstanding. Next contestant?"

John shrunk down in his seat. A moment passed.

"It isn't even that old," Oren continued. "It's from the sixteenth century -- from the *Shulchan Arukh*." He looked at John. "A compilation of Jewish law by Rabbi Yosef Karo."

Thanks. Everyone else knew this? What about Jew-lee?

"It says you can't eat fish and meat together because it causes leprosy. Ridiculous, right?"

"But it's still *halacha*," Naomi said, which, John could tell, was somehow supposed to be for his benefit.

"I'm not saying it's not," Oren said. "But the *Shukhan Arukh* also says you can't drink water from a container that was left open overnight. Why? In case a snake got into it. I'm serious. Tell me you wouldn't drink water from an open bottle? I mean, you might not. Just not because of *halacha*. But no surf and turf?"

"Lobster's not kosher," Julie said.

"Yeah, smart guy," Neal added, mockingly pointing at Oren's face.

"I don't mean it literally."

"Well, I thought it was about the fish bones, too," Naomi said. "Oren likes the minutiae."

John smiled shyly. *Was that pity? Girls don't go for guys based on pity. No Saklahar-whatever in public school. Alma Moses.* John realized he was staring at a piece of challah in his hand. How long had he been doing that? *Cha-lah.*

"It's not minutiae," Oren said. "If people say you're not *supposed* to do something, how often do you think they really know why? How often are they even right about what the '*supposed* to' is? Most of the time, they're just repeating someone else's mistake or something someone else made up. Come on, even Rabbi Karo made stuff up. He's the guy who said it was okay to use glass dishes for both meat and dairy. Really? How convenient. What do you think was in his cupboard?"

"No one can know everything," Naomi said.

Please stop.

"You're missing the point," Oren said. "All I'm saying is that, yeah, everyone's got their favorite gotcha rule, but for some people, no offense to anyone here, it's only about that." *No offense?* "They hear an obscure rule and get all self-righteous about it -- bragging about following it and catching people who don't."

"What about the red heifer?" Naomi said.

"I knew you were going to say that," Oren said without hesitation. "Why do the ashes of a red cow cleanse someone who touched a dead body? The interpretation is that you're not supposed to understand it. It's because God says so in the Torah. Personally, I think that's a cop out."

"But that just makes everyone else's point," Julie said. *Great.* "You don't have to know everything to participate and presumably, while you shouldn't set out to catch people breaking the rules, you also shouldn't set out to catch people following them either."

"Yeah," Neal said, pointing at Oren again.

Rescued by cha-lah bread.

Oren just smiled.

The conversation continued throughout dinner, but then started to fade at dessert. *Too much wine.* The guests started to glance at their watches. John stood to clear the dessert dishes. Neal and Naomi followed him to the kitchen with dishes and glasses. Oren and Julie found their coats.

"Next time at my place," Neal said. *Next year in Jerusalem.*

John walked them to the door. He noticed Naomi still hadn't put on her coat. As he leaned in to kiss Julie goodnight, Naomi hugged Neal as if she had hosted him herself. She said she was staying to help clean up.

John shut the door. "Thanks for staying. Julie seems nice. Maybe Neal won't screw this up. Go on inside. Sit down." John hurriedly arranged the dishes in the racks of the dishwasher. He wished he could turn it on. His mother used to say the dishwasher made the sound of a night well eaten. He felt that way, too.

He came back into the living room. *Oh, no.*

"I love this one," Naomi said, turning a photo album around to show John.

John laughed. "Must you?"

"You're so cute here."

"I must have been a year old there." *What is it? Three pages in? I can't believe it. Why didn't I get rid of that picture?* Julie reached the page and John could see her quickly glance at the photo then go on. It was a picture of him in front of his family's Chanukah bush -- opening presents. *Mom loved Christmas. Those Goddamn lights. Stockings? How could we?* "You don't want to see the other albums. Oh, come on —"

Naomi pulled John's Bar Mitzvah album from a shelf. *Proof I had one, at least.* She stopped on a black-and-white picture of John with three boys, arms draped around one another.

"Perfect. Now I have 'Stand by Me' in my head," she said.

"If Pluto is a dog, what is Goofy?"

"Could you pick a more obscure quote from the movie? Your bestest-best friends, I assume."

He nodded, but he was thinking about a time when he was ten, when those three friends' mothers got together and decided John was a little too loud -- a little too "hyper-active." They forbid their sons from playing with him for some period. *Six weeks? Six months?* Forever to a little boy. It ended the day he saw the friends playing football in the schoolyard with a bunch of other kids. When he came home and turned on the TV, his mother rattled off a list of kids he should call on. With each name, he told her that that boy too was in the game with his three friends. He described his mood as, *I feel like I have a sickness.*

Without saying a word, his mother drove him to the game and put him in. He learned later, she had then driven to each mother's home and screamed her head off. His friendships with the boys immediately recovered. The mothers' never did.

He hadn't thought about that in a long time.

"Your father is handsome," she said, looking at a picture of the family.

"I hate that picture," John said. "That *yarmulke*. It's the kind they give out in Reform *shuls* because men don't bring their own. It's like the mark of the Reform Jew." *A satin door prize.*

"I'm sure your parents are proud of how much you've learned."

"Mostly they don't know what to do with me. I know they look at me sometimes like I've joined a cult. Their cult, I remind them. But still, I know very little."

There was a pause.

"John, Oren is a jerk. It's easy for him to lecture everyone now about going overboard with *halacha*, because that was what he used to do when he was younger. He was hated. He used to report other kids to the teacher. He even pointed out my parents' mistakes," she laughed. "One Shabbat, we had guests for lunch and they brought flowers. My mother put them in water and Oren started lecturing everyone about not being allowed to water plants on the Sabbath. That wasn't about knowing the origin of a *mitzvah*. That was about a little jerk who couldn't wait to catch someone breaking a rule he'd just learned. He couldn't have planned it better."

Planned it like the fish and meat. Silver cups. A jerk for sure, and probably doesn't help him knowing I'll be in bed with his sister tonight.

"Learning *halacha* is like riding a bike," she said. *Really? You mean it's cliché?* "You can't do it, you can't do it, and then suddenly, you can. And you don't have to think about it anymore. It just becomes a way of life."

Okay, got it. Ready? Turn the knees. Lean forward a bit. Body language.

"Trying to be a good Jew," she said with air quotes. *More like trying to be a Jew.* "It's like trying to hold water in your hands." She cupped her hands and gazed into them. *I like the bike analogy better.* "The water keeps running between your fingers. You keep trying to hold onto it, trying to get your fingers closer together, but you can't. Then suddenly, one day, you realize you've forgotten all about the water and you panic. But when you look down, it's still there. Waiting for you. From then on, every time you look, it's just there. The water." She looked up from her hands. "Sorry, that was really stupid."

Yeah, kind of. "Not at all. It was beautiful." John took her cupped hands, leaned in and kissed her. *Finally.*

John dragged himself from a dreamless sleep. He turned over and stared at the ceiling. *Stay in. Sleep more. When was the last time? Last Sunday. Time? Almost 9:30. Still smell her. Cinnamon? That perfume. What is it again?* He peeled the Band-Aid off his thumb. *Yep. Black. Just near the base. What's that? The cuticle. Yuck. Embarrassing. It might fall off. Toenail did once.* He remembered the soccer play that caused it.

The *shul* was nearly empty. *Should have gotten that share in the Hamptons. Oh well, more* Kiddish *for me.*

John saw Oren sitting near the front. He settled into an empty row near the back and thumbed to a page in a *Siddur. Art*

Scroll. Thank you, Art Scroll. So easy. He read a footnote. *The spice mixture. Galbanum. That's me. We all belong. A local call from here. That's the punch line. What's the joke?*

The murmuring of a small group near John started to grow in volume. *Like a boiling kettle.* The rabbi shushed them. It would happen three or four more times before the end of service. *Always did. Same people, same corner. Why not meet in a park if you want to talk? And there's Martin Lipman. He's the worst of them. Asleep every week. Snores. Gets kicked by someone. Maybe it's an* aliyah? Peticha. *The* aliyah *to open the ark. I think? Mnemonic. Eyes for einai'im.* Petichat einai'im? *The honor of opening the eyes?* He smiled to himself. The Hebrew seemed right. *A joke in Hebrew. Hebglish. Save it.* The congregation stood and John remembered how everyone in his synagogue stood for the recitation of the *Kaddish,* not just those in mourning, like they did at the *shul* he went to now. *Three times a year, Reform Jews stand for those who have no one to stand for them. What's wrong with that? My Bar Mitzvah was in a temple not a* shul. *Temple. Funny word. Like a place to worship a superstition. A Mayan Temple. Incan. Sun god. Isis? Egyptian. But* shul? *Why does that sound okay? Grandma didn't know Yiddish. Chalah bread.*

He turned as a group of men carried the Torah around the sanctuary. *Why do we follow it? Synchronous rotation. Beautiful. Made up?* He recalled Oren's dinner lecture about the origin of *halacha. Is following the Torah in the shulkannawatever? Never turn your back to it? Rabbi Koso? Rabbi Koro? How long till Kiddish? Fifteen page flips until* Musaf. *Additional service. Should be optional service. No Kiddish line with so few people. Maybe chollent? Cold cuts? The Mother of All Kiddishes, Kiddishi? Kiddishim? Focus. Who prays the whole time? Oren? No. He's counting pages, too. Fourteen more flips. It was easier to focus when the service made no sense. Familiarity leads to distraction. Like driving.* Shuls *are noise; temples are silence. Rabbi and an organ. Let's go, Islanders. Don't need page numbers called out anymore. Familiarity. Can read but not understand. Easier to wander. Can always find the way back. The water's still there. Naomi.*

Weeks later, John looked at the black spot on his thumb, which had advanced so much that some white had returned near the bottom. The Band-Aid stayed on whenever Naomi was around.

"I'm hungry."

She was speaking from under the covers. His covers. *A kosher kitchen and a treyf bedroom. It's better than pork, said the rabbi to the priest. Modern Orthodox. Conservadox. Reformodox. Hypocripidox. It's not forbidden. It. Her. Any color as long as it's black. Some kind of paradox. A dilemma. A logic problem. She can only have sex after being in the mikvah, but can't go to the mikvah until she's married, so no sex before she's married. Transitive? Why not expressly forbidden? Can't spill the seed. Onan. Who was Onan? Some jerk off. Oedipus? Some mother fucker. Save those.* He laughed.

"What's so funny?" Naomi asked.

"Nothing. Just glad you're here."

"John," she whined playfully. "I'm still hungry."

"We have nothing." *We.* "Go forage."

She tossed the covers and walked off. He heard the sound of her bare feet on the hard wood floors. *Wrinkle in the sheet. Hair on the pillow. The smell. Her clothes would never be as sexy again. The bed would never be as comfortable. Why? Unintelligent design. The noticing won't last. Everydayness. Riding a bike. It's still there. How long until the extra arm grows in? You're on my hair. How do we start? Silver toys. Kesef. Silver. Yearning. Yearning. Who doesn't yearn? Yearn. Yearn. Yee-urn.*

Bare feet again. He looked at her in his t-shirt. *The refrigerator. A little chill?* "What's the soup?" she asked, holding a bowl.

"It's *milchik*." *Dairy. Sounded comfortable.*

"I didn't ask you that."

"Fake clam chowder."

"Yum."

"But we had chicken two hours ago." *Jagged boundaries. Treyf bedroom.*

"This is amazing."

"Mushrooms instead of clams. It has the same consistency as clam soup." *Uncle Rick. Lobster bake. Bibs.*

She sat at the edge of the bed and slurped cold soup.

"What do you miss most now that you're kosher? Lobster?"

John rested his foot against her back. "Were you reading my mind? I was just thinking about my Uncle Rick and his annual lobster bake. But only because I was thinking about clams. That's so funny."

"So lobster?"

"No. Lobster's just a vehicle to eat butter. Like, wow, I have this nice hot cup of butter and I need to get it into my mouth; I wish I had something to get it there with. I think what I miss most is convenience. It used to be easy to eat. Fast food, street stalls. Not worrying that I ate chicken less than three hours ago."

She stuck out her tongue.

"Totally unrelated," he said, "the Chabad newsletter had a piece about how the silver offered by the Israelites to build the Temple represented the *Baal-Tshuva*, because *Kesef* means silver and also yearning. Gold represented the observant Jews and copper the sinful Jews because it was the lowest of the metals."

"And?"

Can't you pretend like you don't know? "Nothing, was just thinking about it."

"My little Chabadnik." She placed the bowl on the nightstand and slid under the covers next to him. *Curves. Golden Skin. Golden calf. Golden calves. The sound of fingers caressing skin. Or the sound of skin being caressed? Both. Harmony.*

"Let it go," she said at his silence.

"What?"

"The silver thing. They shouldn't group people like that. It's stupid. You have to stop reading the *Chabad* mailer. I swear if you start boiling mites off the lettuce..."

He looked at her impish smile. *Sally sells sea shells.* "It's just. I just feel like a second-class Jew all the time." *Baal-Tshuva. Galbanum. Silver. Yearning.* "No matter what I do, I feel like you guys are real and I'm just faking it. Whatever you want to do, it just seems right. You want to eat *milchik* soup after eating chicken, no one judges it. If I did that, everyone would think I'm giving up or stupid or something."

"Who says no one judges?"

"It's just different. If I do something like that, it's like taking a step backwards and you're just having a little transgression."

"It's all in your head. If anything, I'm judged more because I should know better."

"I get slack like a child?"

"I can't win, can I?"

"No," he said and smiled.

No more Band-Aid. A small black dot floated over the curvature of nail. *Clip. Bite. Gone.* His fingers were wrapped between Naomi's. *It's nothing. A speck.*

They were late for *shul. Lecha Dodi,* The Sabbath Bride, was fading out as they walked in. John brushed Naomi's lips with a quick kiss in the vestibule. A peck. *Goodbye. See you after. There's Oren.* He was sitting in a side pew. John sat with him. *Did he see the kiss? Was Mr. Know-It-All aware that Naomi was planning to sublet her apartment? Weak handshake. Neal's turn to host. About time he made good. Julie was gone. New apartment.*

Ring.

John and Oren's eyes locked.

Oh, no. Crap. No.

Ring.

Who forgets about a cell phone on Shabbat? Baal-Tshuva. Look busy. Sh'ir ha ma'alot, do do do de do do do. Oh wait, that's not right.

Ring.

Shut it off or let it go? Which is worse? A dilemma. No one knows who it is. Oren does. What would he do? It's the attitude.

Ring.

"Shut it off," Oren whispered.

"*It's Muksa,*" John responded. *Can't touch it on Shabbat. MC Hammer. Eyes rolling. Oren's eyes. Stupid. That should be it. Unless someone was leaving a message. Then just beep.*

"Nice place, Neal," John said. "You really didn't pay a broker fee?" *View. Elevator. Doorman. Hard wood. What's the catch? Death? Haunted?*

"Thanks for hosting so soon after moving in," Naomi said. *No really, what's the catch.*

"Your phone off?" Oren said to John.

Asshole. "Sorry about that. Was rushing and just forgot to leave it home." *Heart slamming. Heart. Sweat.*

"It happens, John," Neal said.

"Just don't let it happen at *Shacharit* tomorrow morning," Oren said. *Really? Asshole.* "Because you'll wake up Martin Lipman."

"*P'tikhat einai'im*," John said, looking up. They all laughed. *Oren, my straight man.*

Neal invited everyone to the table for the *Kiddush. Same group. No Julie. One extra setting. Who for?*

"Nell's coming late," Neal said. *Neal and Nell? Cute. Matching tracksuits. I'm with stupid.*

Neal led the prayer and they washed. John brought the challah so he knew he would have to say *Ha'motzi.* He washed and waited in silence for everyone to finish. *Why nervous? Even mom knows this one. And the match-meets-wick prayer. Shel Sha-bat. Shel Chanukah. Shel insert holiday. And the Shemah -- second half. Must have been the organ. Blessed is His glorious kingdom now and forever. Three times a year: Rosh Hashannah, Yom Kippur, Passover. Maybe two. The apathetic parent who screams at the teacher. Job done. Who says I'm not a good mother? Showed her. See you next year. What does a Reform shul do the rest of the year? A resort in the off-season. Death in Venice.*

There was a knock on the door and then the sound of it opening. "Hello?" a woman called into the apartment. No one answered. Neal signaled to John to do the prayer and Nell walked in as he was speaking. He could feel Naomi's eyes leave him to look at her.

"*Barukh atah Adonai Elohaynu melekh ha-olam asher kideshanu b'mitzvotav... I mean... ha-motzi lechem min ha-aretz.*" *Dammit.*

Introductions followed.

Neal's Catholic girl thing. But another Jew? Where does he find them? Oh, the East Side. Of course. Long walk. Through Central Park? Alone? How are you getting home? Right. Bad question.

"This must have fallen," Nell said, handing something to Neal.

Neal looked at it.

The mezuzah.

"I put it up with double-sided tape until I can get someone to drill it in. I'll put it back up."

"Wait," John said.

They looked at him. "Nothing. Just wanted to see it." *Who gets so excited about mezuzahs?* John took it. *Plain. Silver tube. Idiot.*

"*Mezuzah* police," Oren said.

"Just wanted to see it, that's all. Some are pretty nice. Didn't want to make a big deal about it, just wanted to see it, that's all." *I protest too much.*

John handed it to Neal, who disappeared down the hall to reaffix it to the doorpost.

But you can't. We have to go. Can't reside in a home without a mezuzah. Can't affix a mezuzah on Shabbat. Conundrum. The prenuptial Mikva. We must go. What's the right thing to do? He remembered his class. *Fifteen Baal-Tshuvas -- a righteous case study. Scenario analysis. Mezuzahs don't fall down. But what if? And there it was at Neal's new apartment. Neal's temporary mezuzah on the floor in the hallway picked up by his temporary girlfriend. Serial monogamist. A mezuzah fell down on Shabbat. A Baal-Tshuva's dream come true. Winning the halacha lottery. A mezuzah fell down on Shabbat. Nothing more obscure. It's a sign, it has to be; A test. Who would know you can't hang a mezuzah on Shabbat? Only baal-tshuva. Who would know we have to leave? I know. I know.*

John rolled his glass stem slowly between his fingers, staring at the tentacles of light that hung motionless in the wine like compass needles.

Neal came back. "Ready to eat?" He was already bringing in plates of food. Nell was being asked questions about herself.

Look interested. Act interested. Oren should have been all over it. The *mezuzah. There must be a loophole. Some ambiguity. Maybe if people are in the house already. Maybe the mezuzah in the kitchen counts. Emitting mezuzahness. A mezuzah radio tower. Electricity? The walls all touch. Red rover, red rover. Kick the can. They already knew the answer. What was it? Can you open the refrigerator on Shabbat? It causes the compressor to turn on when the temperature lowers.*

The mezuzah moment was gone. Should have said something. Why didn't Oren? And is he aware that I'm bedding his sister? Bedding. Martin Lipman. Naomi must have told him to go easy. Preach outreach, practice exclusion. Orthodox parents. The few, the proud, the fearful. Send little Naomi to her aunt's cuz John's coming for Shabbes. Chicken? Hungry. More wine. Tired. Lazy. Comfortable. I'm melting...melting. The fallen mezuzah. Who would leave now anyway? What's the worst that could happen? Disrupt the flow. Game flow. Point guard. Shabbat's an island. Time for family. You want us to leave? No. No distractions. A TV in the kitchen. Just being. Being alone. Alone together.

He caught Naomi's eye and she smiled at him.

Leaving would... would... suck. Contentment. A dilemma. Disrupt Shabbat because the mezuzah fell down. What about the why?

"You know you shouldn't have put the mezuzah back up," Oren said.

John slapped the table hard and laughed. "Dammit, I knew that!"

ABOUT THE AUTHOR

S. Mark Gadol lives with his wife and two children in New York City.